Published in Great Britain in 2016 by Mascot Media (Norfolk) for Rosie Andersen.
Email: mascot_media@btinternet.com
Web: www.mascotmedia.co.uk

www.aelfwynnbooks.com

Email: hello@aelfwynnbooks.com

www.pauljacksonstory.com

Email: paul@pauljacksonstory.com

A CIP catalogue record for this book is available from the British Library.

ISBN: 978-0-9954651-0-7

Written by Rosie Andersen.
Artwork scanning & processing by Mascot Media.

Design and layout by Alan Marshall.
Editing and proofreading by Marion Scott Marshall.

Printed by Swallowtail Print, Drayton Industrial Park, Taverham Road, Drayton, Norwich, Norfolk NR8 6RL.
Email: contact@swallowtailprint.co.uk
Web: www.swallowtailprint.co.uk

For

Kaela, Adam and Finian

with love

Foreword

The traditional Earth-labyrinth represents the explorer's passage through the underworld of the subconscious to reach their spiritual core. Such is the profound nature of the transformation facilitated by this magical ancient artefact of the mind-made tangible.

The journey within is the greatest we can ever undertake. A voyage of exploration into the infinite depths of our own personal psyche, which is sovereign and unique yet part of the whole inter-connected universe – both seen and unseen.

Aelfwynn's sacred journey is our own, and brings to mind the traditional Mayan greeting, 'In Lak'ech Ala K'in', which means, 'I am another yourself'.

We are now inhabiting a time of reconnection with each other, the natural world and the source. In this rediscovery of ancient wisdom we see that we are, as our own ancestors once were, profoundly connected with each other and with all sentient life. Indeed, harmony and concord prevail and flourish on our beautiful blue planet.

Never has a story been so timely as to reintroduce the ancient core wisdom to new audiences both young and old, for the tale of Aelfwynn's path into the labyrinth of her psyche and the natural world will enchant and inform you like no other.

So let us be transported 'beyond the fields we know' into the timeless natural landscape that the author lays before us as a veritable feast to nourish our famished souls...

Dr Ian C Baillie

Preface

This is a tale for the seeker, the adventurer, the inquirer and the curious. At its simplest, it is a tale about walking amongst trees and in woods. In addition, it is about being aware of one's surroundings and noticing the myriad happenings within nature, from the miniscule to the immense. It is also written as a tale full of metaphors for the reader to explore personally, to follow the journey and find their own meanings.

The story developed from six song-like passages, and is a mixture of personal experiences, real places and observations, together with myth and make-believe. It involves Aelfwynn's (and our own) experience of walking a labyrinth, often thought of as an allegory for life. With its twists and turns, we sometimes appear to be existing on the edge; yet at other times feeling secure and close to our centre. It mirrors our passage through time, living within a large, all-encompassing and complex ecosystem taking us through the contrasting cycles of nature – symbols of our ever-changing lives. All is on the move: conditions change, circumstances unfold, nothing stands still. As it is being contained within the labyrinth, so it is within our lives. We are never truly lost, but neither can we work out or predict exactly where we are going, only that at some point we will reach our centre, the heart of it. During this journey we may walk quickly, take our time, or stop and reflect. We may feel sad or joyful, encountering a range of emotions and feelings. However long it takes us, the same path that draws us in will lead us out again. The practice of walking a labyrinth entails entering with our troubles, burdens and questions; contemplating, meditating or praying at the labyrinth's centre; and then going back out into the world in the hope of feeling more able to cope with life's challenges.

The tale also includes the presence of Jack-in-the-Green, a mysterious, though light-of-heart, 'Robin Hood'-type character associated with May Day celebrations past and present. Jack is also known as the 'Green Man', a pre-Christian nature spirit – a symbol of inspiration. In addition, he can represent our relationship with nature and God or the Divine who, in Aelfwynn's story, welcomes her, invites her to follow him, watches over her, and finally asks her not to forget him.

Rosie Andersen

SONGS OF THE TREES

Aelfwynn's Journey into the Labyrinth

"Trees are sanctuaries. Whoever knows how to speak to them, whoever knows how to listen to them, can learn the truth. They do not preach learning and precepts, they preach undeterred by particulars, the ancient law of life."

Hermann Hesse (Bäume: Betrachtungen und Gedichte, 1984)

Deep within the WOOD, if listening carefully, can be heard the
rich, resonant and tonal voices of the TREES as they sing
their songs to each other, to us and to the Universe -
SONGS to awaken our SPIRIT.

But only those who are SILENT can hear.

For the trees are MESSENGERS for humanity, healing and
supporting us when all else worldly has failed.

Through their songs, each tree amplifies its qualities and virtues -
communicating PEACE and LOVE to the world.

LISTEN ... and we will find our answers.

Aelfwynn, though born into a human family, was not only elf-like in name but, curiously, in appearance too. She was blessed with kindness, patience, tolerance and care that shone through into everything that she did and her interactions with others. Over time, though, there had been people in her life who had not been so thoughtful and kind towards her and who had taken advantage of her good nature. However, her goodness and virtues had not gone unnoticed by the trees she loved to visit.

Repeatedly drawn to the woods and forests, Aelfwynn always felt at home there where she could experience the elements that made her feel alive and vibrant. Spending time within nature provided the solace she needed, away from the sensory overload witnessed daily in her world.

One day, after feeling she had lost her sense of belonging, she visits the sacred grove. Bringing her life's troubles and worries with her, an extraordinary journey takes place – walking a labyrinth, travelling to the centre of her being, healing her sadness and changing her life forever.

"I only went out for a walk and finally concluded to stay out till sundown, for going out, I found, was really going in."

John Muir (John of the Mountains: the unpublished journals of John Muir, 1938)

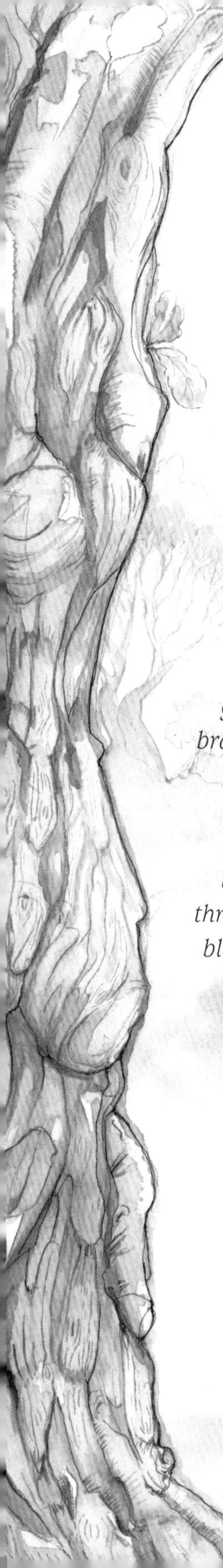

Two large oaks stood at the entrance to the wood. They were the guardian trees of this magical place, inviting and enticing all to enter. Aelfwynn stood silently in between the two trees, her hands resting gently on the bark. She knew this wood very well, and was inspired by the flora and their colours that transformed the look and feel of it throughout the changing seasons.

In autumn, the light shone softly through the leaves, though still with radiance and a golden glow, picking up the changing colours of the surrounding vegetation. Shafts of light would flash and flicker through the woodland canopy as the breeze moved and shifted the foliage. Numerous spider webs gleamed in the trees; and, when lying on the woodland floor gazing up at the moving sky, limitless shimmering webs interconnected the branches. The ground would be deep in leaves from previous seasons, providing a prolific and sumptuous covering to lie or sit upon.

As winter approached with its cold, crisp air, there was a feeling of space, timelessness and anticipation. One could see far into the heart of the wood through the bare branches which, in the pale light, hung like skeletons, bare and bleak. The growth on the woodland floor was now dormant where little stirred and all appeared to sleep.

In spring, the life force would once again awaken, glimpses of growth appearing with browns changing to greens and all around an atmosphere of expectation and movement. Lichens of varied sizes and hues would begin to spread over the woodland floor with the ammonite curls of new bracken growth emerging all around. Listening carefully, you might be conscious of the wary and elusive wildlife. While endeavouring to remain out of sight, they would cautiously watch you from a distance, the occasional hoarse bark of a fox cutting through the tension.

During the summer months, the wood became vital and full of life, everywhere lush, abundant and green, with the forest floor and familiar landmarks obscured by the rich plant-life. Sitting quietly, you might see the deer. If they noticed you, they would freeze and stand motionless for minutes before silently creeping away into the thickets, disappearing completely from view. Rabbits darted out in front of you, swerving so sharply that they were gone barely before you had time to notice their presence. The wood was full of bird song, with sounds everywhere.

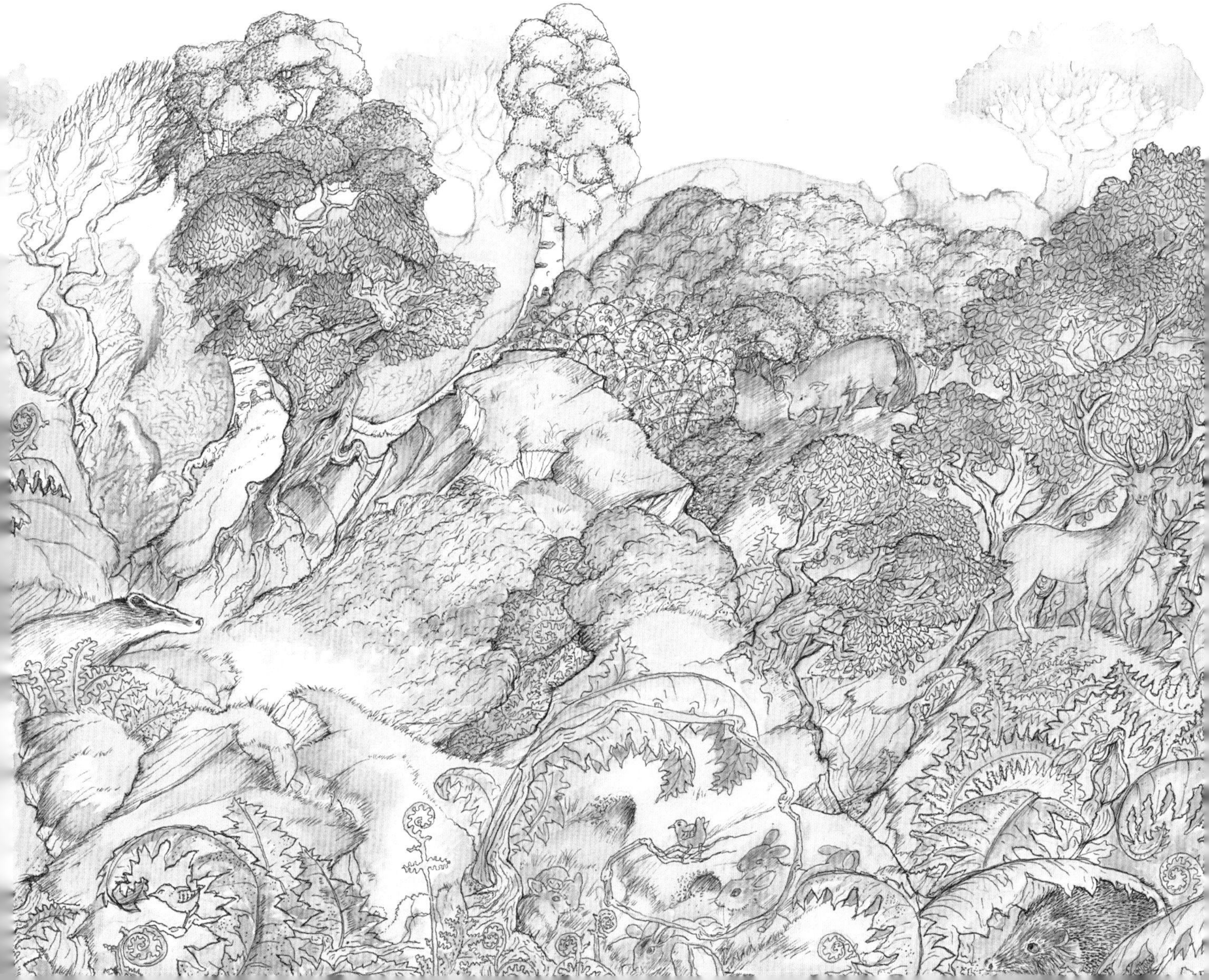

Woods and forests can be both merry and mysterious places. Aelfwynn often felt that the trees were playing mischievous games with her and, at times, creating illusions that caused her to lose her bearings. The tracks created by the deer, which formed their own mazes and networks of narrow paths, could stop as suddenly as they started, vanishing beneath the undergrowth. Despite the denseness of the ground cover, the confusing shadows, the shifting light and the puzzling creaks and cracks, there was a familiarity in the movement and activity of the wood that dispelled any feelings of fear within her. In fact, she was never truly alone. Through this atmosphere of energy and vitality that could even be mistaken for chattering and laughter, Aelfwynn imagined the mercurial and playful presence of Jack-in-the-Green singing to her; whom she felt was there to greet her and watch over her each time she visited the wood.

"Welcome Aelfwynn, I am Jack-in-the-Green."

"Come with me", he murmured,

"come with me", said he.

Welcome to Lwynn
I am
Jack-in the Green
Come with Me
he murmured
Come with me
Said he

On this day it was high summer, warm and still, the air heavy with heat and pollen. Aelfwynn, carrying flowers and four coloured ribbons, walked the path that wound in a convoluted fashion along the outer edge of the wood, the trail twisting and turning at random. It was a relief to enter the shade of the woodland and feel the coolness on her skin. Soon the ground became boggy, as the path crossed an underground spring that caused the area to remain damp all year round. Aelfwynn carefully tiptoed across, trying to avoid the mud. Further beyond the spring and in the centre of the track stood an enormous oak, its vast girth almost filling the space, its presence breathtaking. Despite its immense age, the tree was alive and flourishing, the bark being dense and gnarled yet tactile and inviting, its deep crevices playing host to numerous creatures that inhabited its hollows. One could not pass without reaching out to touch and connect with this magnificent tree.

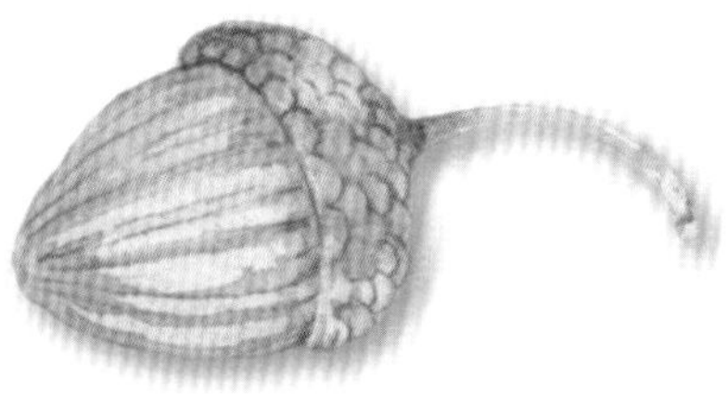

Aelfwynn had been coming to the wood for many years and had, while walking well away from the track, stumbled upon a hidden and untouched space that had become her sacred grove. Here, four oak trees of considerable age and size had gathered, each one marking the four points of the compass. Surrounding these four oaks were other significant trees including tenacious rowans, sporting firstly the white blossoms of spring, and later the red berries of autumn; the undaunted, glossy leaved hollies; and the elegant silver birches with their harlequin bark.

Between these four trees was a clearing. Aelfwynn created a focal point at the centre of the space, and from wood found on the forest floor she formed a rough circle. Within this she placed rings of stones where offerings of flowers could be made.

On the tree in the east, representing the element of air, she tied a yellow ribbon for inspiration, renewal and new beginnings. On the tree in the south, which represented the element of fire, she placed a red ribbon for creativity and transformation. On the tree in the west, representing the element of water, she tied a blue ribbon for cleansing and healing. On the tree in the north, which represented the element of earth, she placed a green ribbon for grounding, support and nurturing. Within the circle of stones at the centre, which represented spirit, she placed flowers.

These were her gifts to the wood and to all the creatures that lived in it.

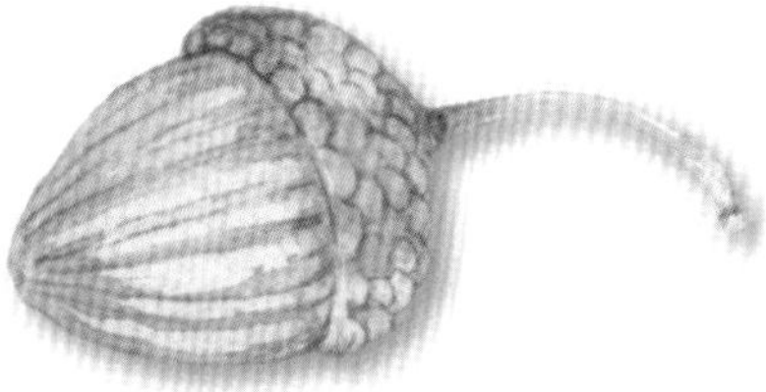

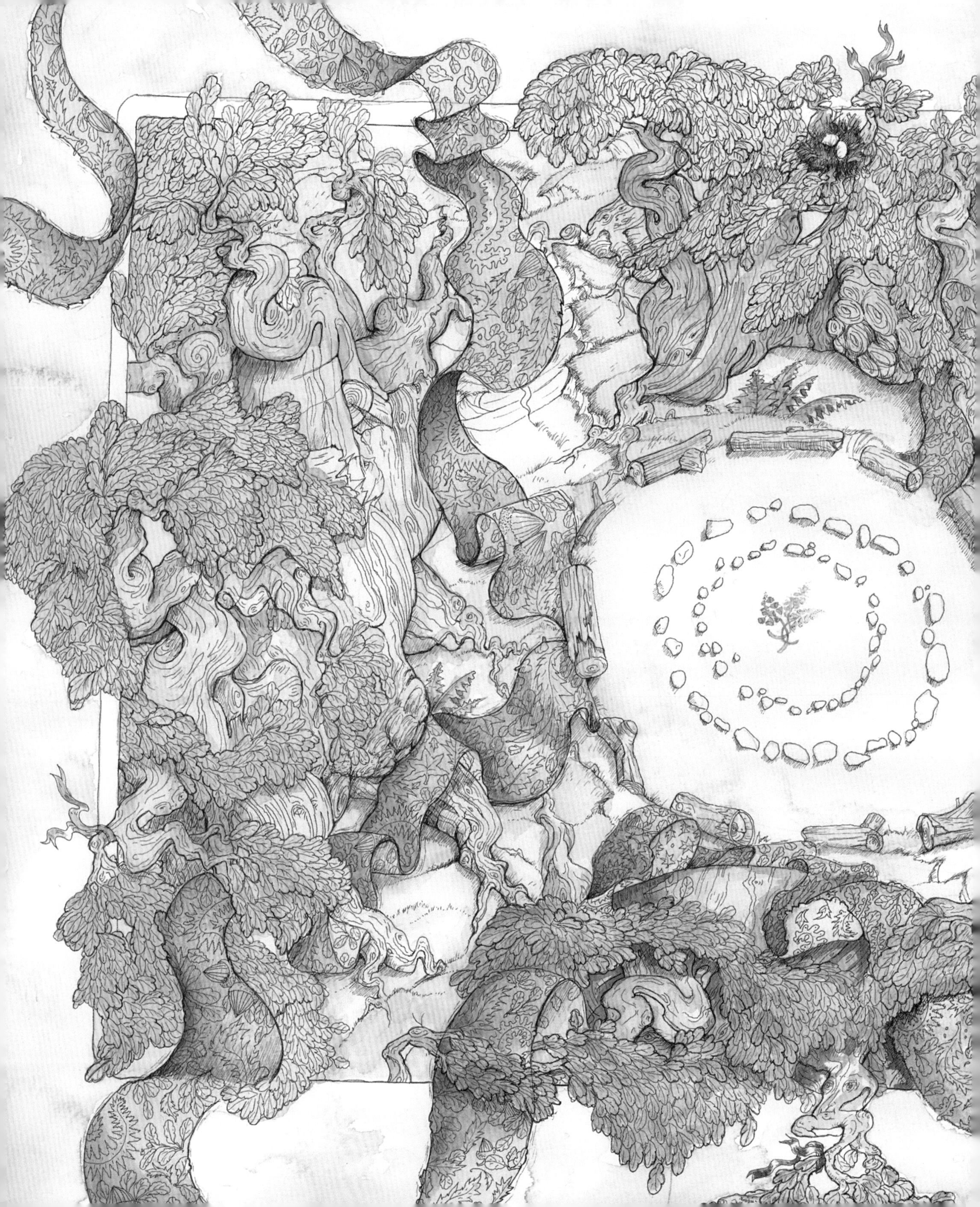

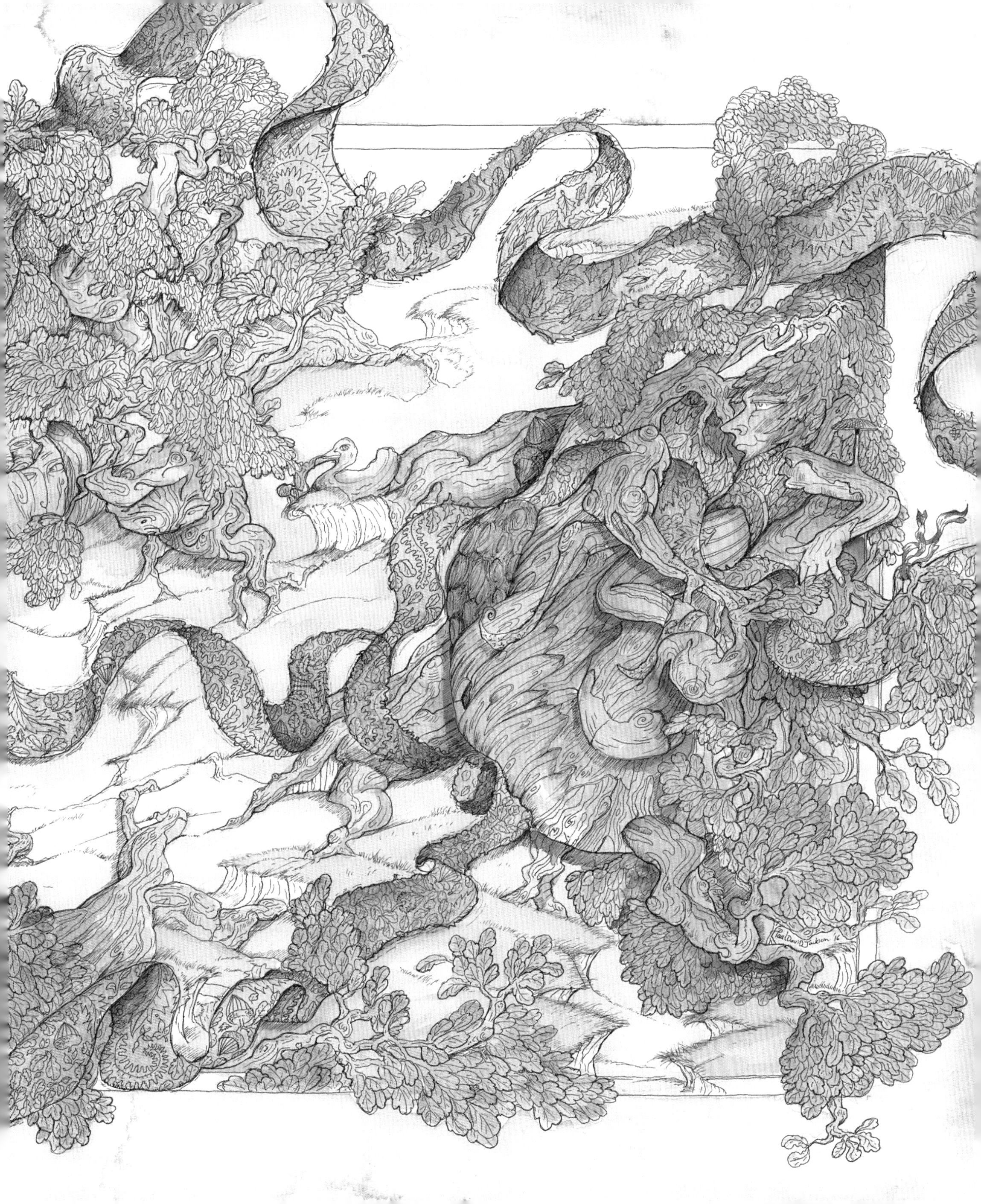
PaulDaviDJackson '16

Aelfwynn continued with her walk along the track through dense unmanaged woodland, eventually reaching an open area surrounded by ripening crops. Hares could be spotted, crouching low in hollows, their ears flattened and held tightly against their bodies. At other times, if disturbed, they would sprint with explosive energy across the fields and grasslands. A narrow flowing river passed through the meadows, bubbling over the stones in the shallows, then opening out into a larger area of deep and clear sparkling water. Aelfwynn entered the pool, immersing herself fully in the cool water. She floated with her face peeping out of the water and soaking up the warm sunshine. She swam through the reeds, passing swans and ducks, with tiny fish darting by her feet and legs. After a while she emerged, drying herself with her dress; and then, lying on the grass, she very soon fell into a deep, dreaming sleep.

FOLLOW
Gaia
Paul David Jackson ©

Upon wakening from her rest in the sunshine, Aelfwynn gathered her thoughts and rose in readiness to leave the wood for the day. She walked towards her usual path – except this time it seemed different. Each side of the track ahead was lined with dense vegetation through which there seemed to be no passable route. Despite the light now being subdued, she was still able to see the path clearly, though the drop in temperature from full sun to shade caused her to shiver. There were, however, other unusual signs that caught her attention. She could see that the leaves on the trees had begun to change colour, and already there were blackberries, rosehips, sloes and crab apples in the hedgerows. Not too far away, she heard he sounds of rutting deer and arking muntjac. If Aelfwynn ad not known the month of the ear, she would have thought hat autumn had arrived early. Despite feeling apprehensive at finding herself in this situation, she was put at ease by being within nature and amongst her friends, the trees, as she imagined the reassuring beckoning of Jack-in-the-Green.

"Follow me", his voice whispered,

"follow me", said he.

Although Aelfwynn had temporarily lost her sense of time, she carried on walking the path and following its meanderings with curiosity. She soon came to realise from the symmetry of the twists and turns that she was in a labyrinth. Here in the wood, she could see how its beautiful form was reflected all around her, in the curling, circling, uncoiling, rippling and swirling patterns within the plant forms, within water and within the animal and insect realms.

Aelfwynn had previously walked small labyrinths in churches and cathedrals and had also walked larger ones that had been cut into turf with others marked by stones and rocks.

She knew from these experiences how beneficial the simple act of walking the winding path of the labyrinth could be, particularly during prayer, meditation and reflection. It had allowed space to listen to her inner voice and glean insights and answers to problems that had been troubling her. Aelfwynn was aware that the focused walking of the labyrinth's path required no decision-making; that only one route was involved that would guide her into the centre and lead her out again safely. So, as she had done many times before, she walked slowly, silently and purposefully, concentrating her thoughts with the help of each step that she took.

"A few minutes ago every tree was excited, bowing to the roaring storm, waving, swirling, tossing their branches in glorious enthusiasm like worship. But though to the outer ear these trees are now silent, their songs never cease."

John Muir (John Muir's California Collection: My First Summer in the Sierra, 1869)

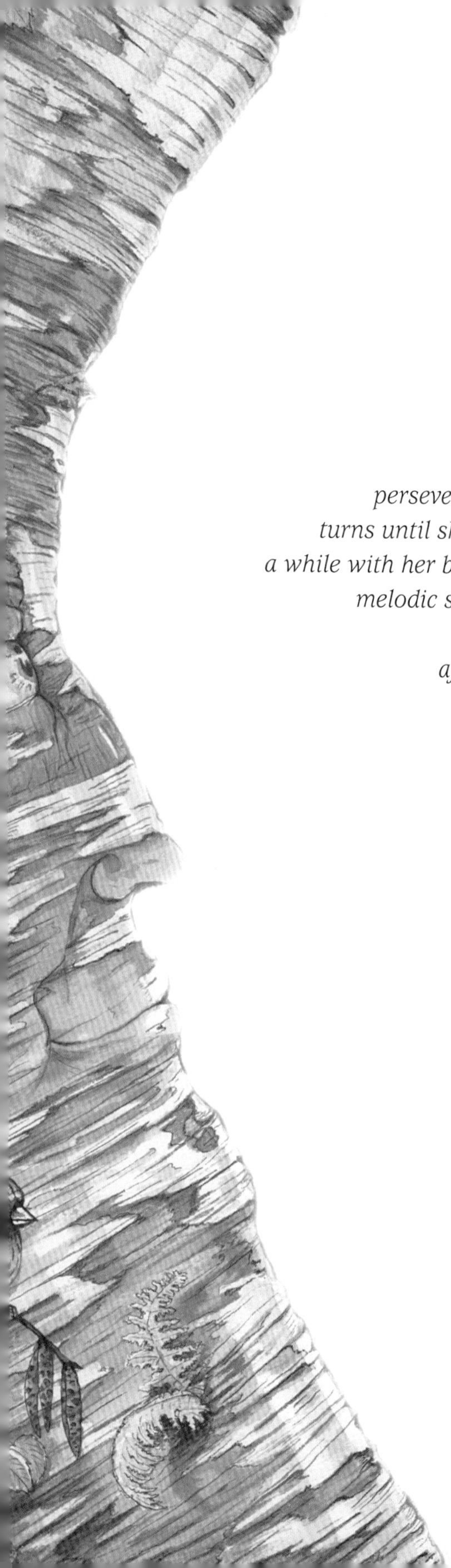

With expectation, Aelfwynn
persevered on her journey – following the trail's many
turns until she came upon a solitary silver birch tree. She sat for
a while with her back against the trunk, and after a time she began to hear
melodic sounds that appeared to be coming from the tree.
She listened until the sounds ceased,
after which a gentle voice began to speak.

"Dearest Aelfwynn, Child of the Forest, I am the Spirit of the Silver Birch tree," the voice whispered. " I am the Lady of the Woods."

"Look for me in the trees, for I am there amongst the muted,
glowing and dappled light.
I am there darting through the leaves
illuminating the glistening spiderwebs whose gossamer threads
float between the branches.

I am there in the crevices of the dense, gnarled
bark of the ancient ones whose leaves provide you with a rich, soft
and springy carpet to walk upon.

I am there in the star-like lichen on the
woodland floor and I am there in the secretive and elusive wildlife,
watching you inquisitively.

For I am there below, beyond, beneath and beside you.
I ... am everywhere."

The voice continued,
"I have heard your call for transformation and growth and I am here to remind you that you can overcome setbacks in your life. I bring you lightness of spirit to help heal your sadness, and I give you hope and new opportunities.
These are my gifts to you."

"Look for me in the trees...

Aelfwynn
thanked the silver
birch tree, which in turn gave her
a small piece of its delicate harlequin bark.

She carried on walking along the path, feeling stronger, calmer and more hopeful, noticing that her surroundings had changed yet again. The leaves had now fallen to the ground, it was cold, frost was forming and the shadows were longer. A pair of tawny owls were echoing each other's calls. Very soon, in the middle of the path, Aelfwynn came across a solitary holly tree with glossy leaves and bright red berries so she stopped to rest and to admire the tree. Once more, she began to hear melodious sounds. She listened attentively until, after a while, the sounds stopped and a crisp, clear voice began to speak.

"Dearest Aelfwynn, Nymph of the Woods, I am the Spirit of the Holly tree," the voice said.
"I am the Protector of the Forest."

"Listen for me in the wind, for I am there amidst the fields and
open spaces, playing within the dancing,
silvered barley and golden wheat.
Hear me in the forests as I gently shift the canopies to and fro,
catching your scent for the hare as she stands
motionless in noble beauty.
I am there in the rivers and lakes, rippling the crystal-clear
velvet waters that caress your skin,
embracing and including you.
For I am there below, beyond, beneath and beside you.
I ... am everywhere."

"I have heard your call for protection and support. This I give you, and I also bring you compassion, love and understanding to help heal your sadness. These are my gifts to you."

Aelfwynn thanked the holly tree, which in turn gave her some of its radiant red berries to keep.

"In every walk with nature one receives far more than he seeks."
John Muir (Travels in Alaska, 1915)

Aelfwynn pressed on walking the track and feeling safe and supported. She became aware of warmer temperatures and increased light. She saw buds bursting on the plants around her with dainty snowdrops and aconites gathering together. Daffodils with their cheerful yellow trumpets were nodding in the breeze, and birdsong could be heard all around. Very soon, she came across a solitary and beautiful rowan tree, shining with its delicate white blossoms. Again she stopped to rest and to admire the tree. She soon began to hear the same melodic sounds, and after a while a gentle voice began to speak.

"Dearest Aelfwynn, Elf of the Trees, I am the Spirit of the Rowan tree," the voice whispered. "I am the Mystic of the Groves."

"Feel for me in the earth, for I am there among the temperate,
the frozen, the parched and the scorched.
I am there in the rich brown soil nestling in the rocks and
waterways, anticipating your every move.
Feel for me between your toes as you walk barefoot
over soft meadow grass and shimmering, shifting sands.
Touch me in the warm sun and chill air as I pass by,
fleetingly, whispering and stroking your face.
For I am there below, beyond, beneath and beside you.
I ... am everywhere."

*"I have
heard your call for clarity
on life's difficult situations, for insight and
protection from negativity. All of these I bring. I also give
you spiritedness and tenacity to help heal your sadness.
These are my gifts to you."*

Aelfwynn thanked the rowan tree, which in turn gave her a sprig of its pure white blossom.

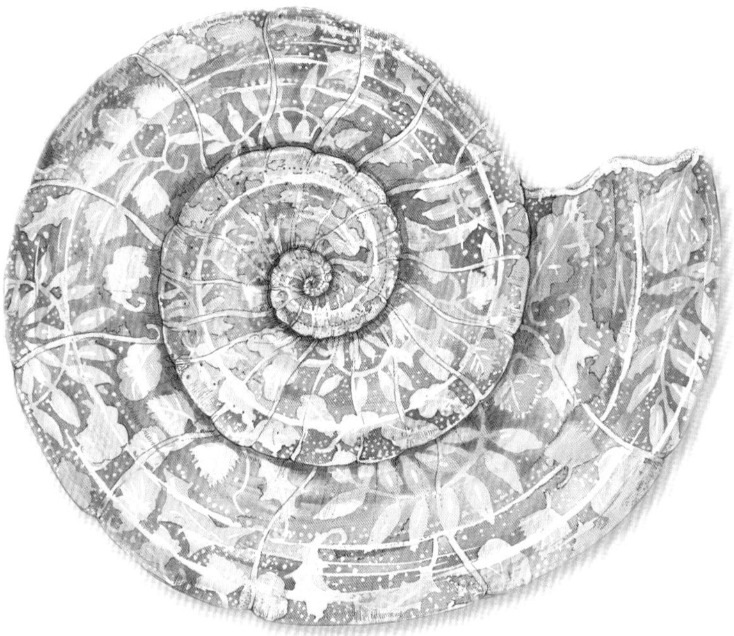

"It is not so much for its beauty that the forest makes a claim upon men's hearts, as for that subtle something, that quality of air that emanates from old trees, that so wonderfully changes and renews a weary spirit."

Robert Louis Stevenson (Forest Notes, 1875/1876)

Her thoughts were now much clearer. She was gaining understanding and feeling happier and more vibrant. As she walked, the season was on the cusp of change from spring to summer. The sun was warm, throwing bright light on to the path. The hedgerows exuded the heady scent of the hawthorn; buttercups danced in the wind; and the hazy, violet blue carpet of wild hyacinths on the woodland floor took her breath away. Further along the track the leaves were in full growth, and all around her were brightly coloured flowers: foxgloves, poppies, willowherb and valerian. Buzzing bees were collecting nectar, and the butterflies flitted from place to place. Swallows swooped and encircled her; a cuckoo could be heard along with the enthralling and hypnotic, sweet song of the nightingale. She had, at last, reached the centre of the labyrinth – and there to welcome her was a stately and majestic oak tree.

*"Dearest Aelfwynn,
Friend of Nature, I am the
Spirit of the Oak tree,
the Sage of the Woods."*

"Think of me when you dance and sing, for I am there
in the movement and sounds kindling your creative imagination.
I am there in the visceral twirls and spins inspiring every step
you take as you enchant and delight.
I am there in your thoughts and words, encouraging you

to communicate your wisdom for others to hear.

Imagine me… for I am there in the silent spaces, helping you to listen; and I am there below, beyond, beneath and beside you.

I … am everywhere."

"I have heard your call for stability and strength. I bring you courage and creativity to help heal your sadness, and I give you self-determination, faith and vision. These are my gifts to you."

Aelfwynn thanked the oak tree, which in turn gave her a perfect acorn to plant.

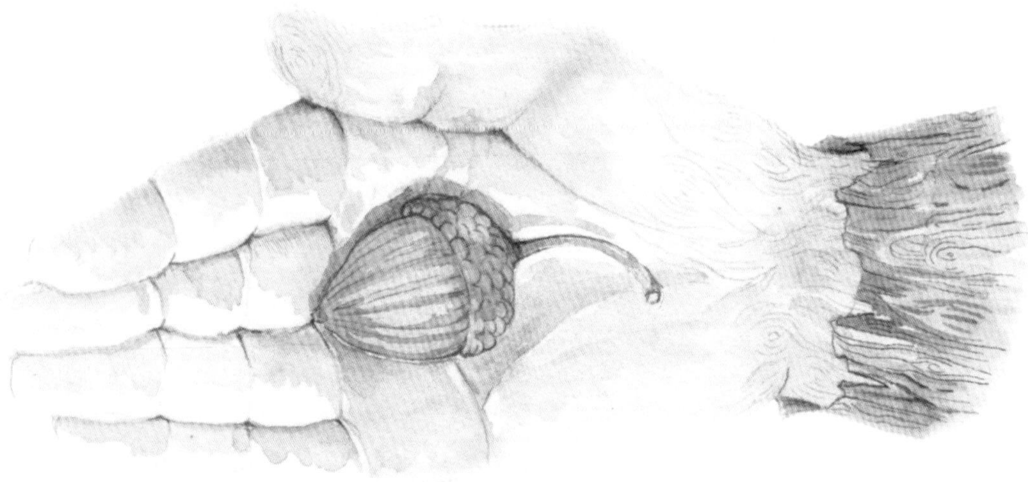

*The silver birch,
the holly, the rowan and the
oak then all began to sing to her a
beautiful song in celebration of
her memorable journey.*

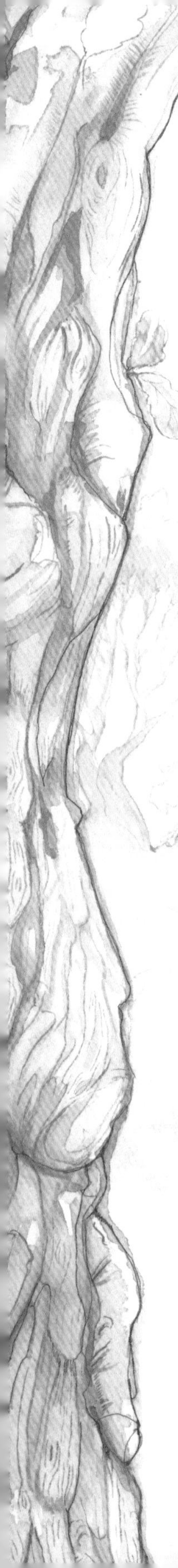

"Dearest Aelfwynn,
you have walked a path of deep communion,
treading softly on this earth.
Your journey has spiralled towards the centre of our shared
experiences, conversing, confiding, celebrating.
You do not walk alone.

With us you discover your creativity,
affirming your divinity and wisdom,
surrendering to the joy of cherished rapport.

You have walked immersed in the colours of the seasons,
with trust, unity, harmony and fellowship.
On this journey we have walked beside you
to that sacred space of sanctuary
with affection, affinity and acceptance.

You have dared to dance in the delight of our connection
where, onwards, to this place of belonging,
You Walk."

Aelfwynn, with renewed energy and positivity, her sadness gone and feeling peaceful, safe and secure, began walking once more, this time to leave the labyrinth and the wood. With an unexpected gust of autumnal wind, a flurry of leaves scattered around her. She smiled, knowing she belonged again.

As she passed between the two guardian trees, she clearly heard fading into the distance the kindly voice of Jack-in-the-Green.

"Forget me not", he whispered,

"forget me not", said he.

PAINTING DA

Yesterday w
Silver Birch
Today an
ammonite.
I try the sha
over and over
pencil and realise
how difficult it is to
draw something that natu
has already made perfect. At last
it is in balance and I mark out the patterns.
A wash of translucent orange, chrome
yellow and verde oliva brings the
image to life. The picture is
complete. Tomorrow it's my
page. Maybe there could be
a spider's web to reflect
the ammonite's shape? I
imagine I'll paint a wash of
foxgloves – perhaps the wren that lives
in my garden could feature, too – and as
I begin drawing the picture starts
to come to life, just as it did when
I drew for the first time. A
tightrope of webs, a bright
light, colourful people following
a spiralled path out from its centre and
into the world...

Paul's Story

I first met Rosie when I was performing an evening of stories in Suffolk. She enjoyed the stories, and was intrigued that the press release described me as a storyteller and artist. She visited my website to look at my illustrations, liked the style, and asked if I might be interested in a book she had written. A few weeks later, we met in a coffee house in Norwich where she read 'Songs of the Trees' to me.

I was there at once in Aelfwynn's magical forest. From the first time I climbed up into a tree I've been enchanted by them. To a small, imaginative boy they seemed like very old people, all wrinkled with great girths and huge spreading arms.

It was September when I began illustrating Rosie's book. I remember it was the time of the first ripe blackberries. I had decided on a certain passage from the book, "She could see that the leaves on the trees had begun to change colour, and already there were blackberries, rosehips, sloes and crab apples in the hedgerows". I took some of this colourful splendour home to draw and help me find the look of Aelfwynn… I drew her then, dressed in those leaves and colours, and in doing that her face slowly formed on the sketching page, along with the palette of colours I would use.

So for every illustration during the next 18 months, I would sit in my workshop and re-read. Certain passages captured my imagination and became the ones I would illustrate. For instance, in The Mischievous Forest, I wanted to depict how forests seem to change even though we think we might know them well.

When I came to paint the Great Oak, I felt this was the essence of Aelfwynn's story; she meeting the Great Oak in all its wonder – vast, gentle and somehow deeply wise. In my quest to find and paint this tree, one morning I headed up to my local wood at Lion's Mouth, wandered among the 400-year-old great oaks and then sat quietly in their grove. Rushing home afterwards to quickly draw the essence of an oak in my imagination that was to become the cover of this book.

Because of its importance to the story, I felt quite nervous when I emailed the finished painting to Rosie a week later. However, I was more than a little surprised and delighted when, a few minutes later, she responded with, "How did you do that? That's my oak tree from my forest!".

The successful relationship between an author and the illustrator is a difficult one to describe, but when it works like it has done for 'Songs', it's a wonderfully enriching experience.

Aelfwynn's journey in 'Songs' was my journey, too. Reconnecting me with nature, with magical trees and with the small, imaginative boy who went climbing many years ago.

Travel Lisbon International Guide

Cecelia .Q Hutchinson

Introduction

Lisbon, Portugal's vibrant capital, beckons you to explore its wonders, and with this ultimate tourist guide, your Lisbon adventure has never been easier. Let's begin our journey by discovering the various modes of transportation to navigate this charming city.

Traveling around Lisbon is a breeze, and you have several options at your disposal. You can choose to explore the city by car, and we'll provide you with the best driving routes and day trip ideas that will allow you to uncover the beauty of the Lisbon region.

If you're wondering whether to rent a car for your Lisbon trip or not, we'll weigh the pros and cons to help you make an informed decision. But if you prefer to explore the city on foot, we've got you covered with tips and insights on the best walking routes and must-see attractions.

For efficient and budget-friendly travel within the city, Lisbon's metro system is a fantastic choice. Learn about metro prices, ticket types, and how to ride the iconic tram, an essential Lisbon experience. We'll also guide you through Lisbon's taxi services for your convenience.

Traveling is about making the most of your trip, and our travel tips will ensure a smooth and enjoyable experience. Discover essential advice for first-time travelers and how to avoid common tourist gimmicks. Plus, find packing essentials to prepare you for your Lisbon adventure.

Budgeting is a crucial aspect of any trip, and we'll help you plan accordingly. Learn about the most economical seasons to visit Lisbon, budget-friendly accommodations, and affordable ways to explore the city on foot.

Creating an itinerary is key to experiencing all that Lisbon has to offer. Our guide will assist you in planning your days and exploring Lisbon year-round. Discover annual festivals and events, from the New Year's Concert in January to seasonal activities that make Lisbon a delightful destination.

As we delve deeper into Lisbon's treasures, explore must-see attractions, iconic streets, and hidden city secrets. Uncover the local gems and natural beauties that grace this magnificent city. Lisbon's culinary scene is not to be missed, and we'll introduce you to the best traditional food, restaurants, bars, and markets where you can savor the flavors of Lisbon.

For those considering settling in Lisbon, we'll provide insights into vacation accommodations, the pros and drawbacks of expat living, and the benefits and challenges of making Lisbon your new home.

With this book, you'll have all the tools and knowledge needed to make the most of your Lisbon adventure, creating unforgettable memories in this enchanting city.

Contents

CHAPTER ONE
TRAVELLING AROUND LISBON

Lisbon is home to a sizable, practical, reasonably priced, and user-friendly public transit network. There are several ways to move around this little city, including buses, trams, underground subway trains (referred to as the metro), and ferries that bridge the river. Generally speaking, taking public transportation is more convenient than renting a car if you intend to stay in the city the entire time you are traveling. Furthermore, using the rail or bus will be lot simpler (and less stressful) than having to drive and maybe encountering heavy traffic, depending on where you need to go outside of Lisbon. In order to save time and money, it is ideal to become at least somewhat familiar with Lisbon's public transportation system before visiting.

By foot and public transportation, you can navigate Lisbon the best. You can explore the city on your own two feet, but keep in mind that traversing the city's hilly streets on foot can be quite a workout.

Think about using the bus, tram, subway, and elevators for a change of pace (and to catch your breath). *One word of warning: Santa Justa Elevator and Tram 28 in Lisbon are both attractions, so expect crowds*. Think about taking a taxi for a faster trip. Just be aware that due to the traffic during rush hour, you will spend some time sitting in your cab. The Lisbon Portela Airport (LIS), which is located about 3 miles north of the popular tourist areas in the city center, has an exceptionally large supply of taxis. The average cost of a taxi to the city center is between 10 and 15 euros, or around $12 and $19 USD. Additionally, the airport has a subway station with a direct route to the city's center. In around 20 minutes, the Aeroporto-Saldanha line will take you into the heart of Lisbon.

There are several different modes of transportation available in Lisbon, including the metro, buses, trams, funiculars, trains, taxis, and tuk tuks, in addition to free walking tours. Vania Silva, a local expert from Free Tours by Foot Lisbon, reveals to you the best routes to and from the Lisbon Airport, as well as some insider knowledge to help you move around the city like a local.

CAR

We don't advise renting a car because it can be difficult to find parking and navigate traffic, especially in the popular downtown areas. Thankfully, the majority of the city's top attractions are accessible on foot, via bus, tram, and train. You can rent a car from kiosks at the airport and from businesses in the city center if you're going on a day trip. You can use your American driver's license, but it might be a good idea to get a DMV.org or AAA international driver's permit.

Lisbon is incredibly congested, making driving challenging and even dangerous; the city has an abnormally high accident rate. Lisbon always seems to be in rush hour. (Theoretically, rush hours are 8–10 am, 1–2 pm, and 4–6 pm on Monday–Friday.) It seems impossible to park. Do not rent a car until you are leaving the city on an excursion. If you're driving into Lisbon from another town or city, call your hotel ahead of time and inquire about the closest garage or alternative parking options. Until you're ready to leave, leave your car there.

THE BEST DRIVING ROUTES OF THE LISBON REGION

- Serra da Arribida and the N379

The Serra da Arribida hills provide a stunning backdrop for the N379. This route is the most scenic in the Lisbon area.

The route meanders through the hill and travels through old trails. One particularly dramatic segment of the road crosses a high ridge and offers breathtaking views to the north and south. Numerous stops along the way allow travelers to pause and take in the breathtaking panoramas of the sado Estuary's turquoise waters and the Portinho da Arrabida's idyllic beaches. The lovely beach town of Sesimbra and the Cabo Espichel Headland, which is home to dinosaur footprints, should both be seen on a day trip along the N379.

- From Azoia to Cascais via the N247

The N247 winds its way along the rocky coast to the north of Cascais, passing the sizable surfing beach of Guincho before ascending into the Serra de Sintra highlands. The route is peaceful, picturesque, and passes by numerous classic Portuguese villages, in addition to offering many breathtaking perspectives.

The most westerly point in Europe, the Cabo da Roca Headland, the Peninha Viewpoint, the breathtaking beach of Praia da Ursa, and the quaint seaside hamlet of Praia das Maccás might all be included in the driving tour. Few international tourists are aware of this highly excellent driving day trip.

- Going across the bridge at Ponte 25 de Abri,

Crossing the Ponte 25 de Abril suspension bridge is the best way to enter Lisbon. This magnificent bridge spans the Tejo Estuary at its narrowest point and towers over the city. Despite only being a 2-kilometer drive, the bridge crossing will make for one of your most memorable drives in Lisbon.

The Cristo Rei monument, which overlooks Lisbon and the A2 countries to both the Serra da Arrabida and the Costa da Caprica coastlines, is located on the southern side of the Tejo Estuary.

Avoid crossing during the evening rush hour or on weekends when everyone is returning from the beaches, as the Ponte 25 de Abril experiences terrible rush hour traffic, especially while traveling north due to the toll station.

- Cascais via the N6

From Lisbon to Cascais, the N6 follows the coastline towards the west. This path passes numerous stunning beaches (Carcallelous, Oeiras, and Torre). Although the N6 is a congested road, there are numerous opportunities to detour and take in the scenery.

THE BEST DAY TRIPS WITH A CAR

You can travel to more areas during day trips if you have a car. Here is a list of our recommended multi-stop day journeys from Lisbon that can only be accomplished by automobile.

- Lagoa de Bidos, Buddha Eden, Obidos, Foz do Arelho, or

The typical walled town of Portugal is Obidos, but it is merely a little village that can be explored in less than two hours. Visits to the historic beach town of Foz de Arelho and the unspoiled Obidos laggon could be included in a day trip to the Obidos region. The Buddha Eden is an alternate destination; it is a quiet parkland that houses the greatest collection of Buddha statues in Europe.

- Mafra and Ericeira.

One of Portugal's most impressive royal structures is the enormous Mafra palace, but after spending two hours inside, there isn't much more to see in the town. We advise pairing Mafra with Ericeira, a hip surfing destination. There are numerous beautiful beaches in Ericeira where you can go surfing or just watch the surfers. The town also offers charming fishing neighborhoods.

The National Palace of Mafra in Mafra village close to Lisbon.

Ericeira Background Portugal

- Evora

The Alentejo region's historic capital, Evora, has undergone very little change from its peak in the 16th century. Along with a room temple, a Gothic cathedral, and an old university building, the area has cobblestone alleys lined with traditional homes. Evora's attractions may fill a full day, but a tour could also include a stop at Cromeleque dos Almendres, a Neolithic stone formation.

Evora background

SHOULD I RENT A CAR FOR MY LISBON TRIP?

If you're debating whether to rent a car for your vacation to Lisbon, base your decision on this:

- If this is your first visit to Lisbon, it is not advisable to rent a car.
- It is a brief journey of fewer than four days (and you will be visiting the main sights).
- If you are under 25 or if this is your first time driving in Europe, there are unfair and prohibitive surcharges for young drivers.
- If you lack confidence behind the wheel,

- ✓ If you plan to spend more than six days in the Lisbon region, we advise renting a car.
- ✓ If your home is located outside of the city and far from the primary transportation hubs,
- ✓ Enjoy exploring off-the-beaten-path locations and non-tourist attractions.

Driving in Lisbon is not fun, so you should seriously evaluate whether you need a car while visiting the city.

There is a severe lack of parking and very congested, narrow roadways in the historic center.

It doesn't get any better on the roads once you get to the expressways. Many of the connections are quite complicated and have subpar signage, and some of the roads have very bad surfaces. The expressways improve as you learn how to use them, but the first few times are tense and it is incredibly simple to get lost.

Always keep a reliable GPS or navigation app on your phone.

While just visiting Lisbon, there is no need for a car because the public transportation is good and taxis and Uber are reasonably priced. There is excellent public transportation to the well-liked day outings, including Sintra, Cascais, or the beaches along the Estoril coastline.

BY FOOT

If your hotel is situated in one of the Chiado, Rossio, or Baixa neighborhoods, you can stroll to the majority of downtown attractions. Just make sure you have some endurance and a nice pair of sneakers. It's preferable to use public transportation to get to areas like Belém, which are about 6 miles west of the tourist area and situated atop some high hills, as well as Bairro Alto and Alfama.

METRO

The subway is more practical for getting around outside of downtown than inside of it. The four colored metro lines stop at 55 stops. Every day from 6:30 a.m. to 1 a.m., the metro is in service. Every 6 to 9 minutes, trains run. The green line connects the tourist regions around Baixa and the train station to Cascais. The red line runs from the airport to Expo Park and other lines. The yellow and blue lines, which follow Lisbon's major thoroughfares, are more frequently used by locals than by visitors. A day pass, which includes buses, trains, and trams, costs 6.30 euros, or less than $8, while a single ticket for the subterranean metro costs 1.45 euros, or $1.80. All public transportation, including the metro, is available for free and unlimited travel if you have a Lisboa Card.

Lisbon Metro Station

METRO'S PRICES AND TICKET TYPES

Lisbon's metro system has two fare zones, but zone one includes the airport and all of the major tourist attractions. Tickets for the Lisbon metro can be bought with cash or a credit card. The cost for a single ride is 1.50 euros, while a 24-hour unlimited travel pass costs 6.40 euros. All buses and trams in Lisbon are included in this ticket.

When compared to buying a prepaid card, buying your ticket onboard is more expensive. For buses and trams, one-way on-board fares are 2 and 3 euros, respectively. Although there aren't any official "round-trip" tickets, numerous single tickets can be bought for back-to-back trips.

You will encounter signs like "correspondência" (which directs you to change lines) and "sada" when using the metro (the exit to the street).

✓ A day passes

Lisbon's day passes for the city's buses, trams, and metro allow for unlimited travel over the whole 24-hour period and cost 6.40 euros. This is the best and most convenient option if you intend to make more than five trips on the bus or subway in a single day.

✓ Viva la Vida

The "Viva Viagem," a reusable transit card, is another way to pay for transportation in Lisbon. It can be used to hold a variety of metro tickets, including numerous single fares, the 24-hour pass, and "zapping" credit, and costs 50 cents for the initial purchase. It's significant to remember that, in contrast to other cities, each passenger needs a separate Viva Viagem ticket.

The card is used twice during each journey: once when you enter the metro station and once when you leave the final metro station.

- ✓ Zapping

If you want to use public transit but do not require a 24-hour ticket, you can purchase a "zapping" ticket, which permits credit to be applied to the Viva Viagem card, which can be used to pay for all forms of public transportation. The zapping prices cost 1.34 euros instead of 1.50 euros, which is marginally cheaper than the standard ticket price.

Additionally, zapping tickets can be used on ferries or suburban trains (without the need to purchase another Viva Viagem card). This makes it possible to skip the lengthy lines at the train terminals. At any metro ticket machine, the Viva Viagem card can be loaded with anything from 3 to 40 euros.

THE TRAM: HOW TO RIDE IT

Lisbon has over 60 trams, often known as streetcars or trollies, that travel along five different routes. Every day, both locals and tourists ride the tram, which may get quite packed during rush hours. The tram stations are well indicated throughout the city with a little yellow (paragem) sign that is suspended from lampposts.

The city's trams, especially the well-known "nostalgic" number 28, are a popular tourist attraction because they are often old streetcars. This well-liked yellow wooden tram goes through a number of attractive neighborhoods along the city's winding, narrow streets, making it a must-ride for tourists who want to unwind and take it all in. It is a six-mile route that connects Bairro Alto and the well-known So Jorge Castle. It travels through a number of urban districts, such as Alfama, Baixa, Chiado, and others.

The best place to board tram 28 is at Miradouro das Portas do Sol (and take it through to Estrela Basilica). Due to the popularity of this tram, standing room only is the norm for most of the day.

It's simple to get to the Belem area from downtown by using tram number 15. You have a choice of starting your journey in Comercio Square or Figueira Square (and getting off at Jeronimos Monastery).

TRAM FARES

A single ticket can be purchased for 3 euros in cash only onboard the tram.

Extra Ticket Choices

Another option is to purchase the 24-hour public transportation ticket, a bundle that also gives access to bus and metro services (along with the funiculars and the Elevador de Santa Justa, a major tourist spot in the city). This ticket must be purchased at a metro station and costs 6.40 euros.

The new CAF tram for Lisbon

Both the traditional "Remodelado" tram and the contemporary Siemens "Articulado" tram are available in Lisbon. When purchased on board, tram tickets cost €3,00.

The Remodelado trams are the postcard-perfect yellow trams that rattle and screech along Lisbon's winding streets. Tram 28E, which travels through the Alfama neighborhood, is the most picturesque route. The Remodelado trams can hold 24 passengers with almost the same amount of standing room, and they are frequently crowded. Please be mindful of your surroundings and possessions when using the tram. Like any major city, Lisbon does experience a small pickpocket problem, especially in busy and tourist areas (including the bus, metro, and tram). Known for having a pickpocket issue, Tram 28

Although they only run along the 15E route linking central Lisbon to the Belem neighborhood, the Articulado trams are significantly larger and less constrained. The best way to get to Belem is with the 15E tram. Belem is a well-liked tourist area with quite a few attractions, including the well-known Pasteis de Belem.

Three funiculars and an elevator from the 19th century still function in Lisbon. These are used by visitors and some locals and are situated in the steep areas of the city where the metro doesn't go. The cost of the Santa Justa Elevator is €5.30, and the funiculars to Bica, Glória, and Lavra are each €3.80. (valid for two trips).

LISBON'S TAXIS

When you need to get from point A to point B, sometimes taking a taxi is the best option. Fortunately, taxis in Lisbon are surprisingly affordable for navigating around the city. Always choose the taximeter because it is required by law for all taxi prices to be computed using one. Typically, the metered trip is more expensive than the predetermined fee. Every time you board a cab throughout the day, you must pay the minimum fare of €3.25, which is due immediately. Every 24 seconds, there is a first increment of €0.10 (after the first 1,800 meters). The minimum purchase amount on weekends, holidays, and at night (after 20:00) is €3.90. The additional charge stays the same (but starts after the first 1,400 meters). Interestingly, there are additional expenses as well. For instance, the luggage price is €1.60 and the fee for telephone reservations is €0.80.

The charges are substantially higher, and the passenger is responsible for paying tolls if they take a taxi outside of the municipal limits, like to Sintra.

Taxi cabs in Lisbon

TRAVEL TIPS

When planning a vacation to a destination like Lisbon, you must take a lot of factors into account in order to avoid running into unforeseen difficulties. Traveling is a very delightful and enjoyable component of a person's life, as well as that of their family, friends, and coworkers, thus it must be well planned to make it unforgettable. Some recommendations to implement include

Tips for first-time travelers before they depart

Tourist gimmicks

Budgeting

TIPS FOR FIRST-TIME TRAVELLERS BEFORE THEY DEPART.

Arrival: Over 30 airlines frequently fly into Lisbon's Portela Airport, which serves as Portugal's primary international hub. Taxis and Uber are widely available and cost approximately 15 euros for the fastest route to your hotel. The Metro (a 25-minute ride on the red line connecting through Saldanha station) and buses, which have several routes that serve the city, are the most reasonably priced options to travel to Lisbon's city center.

Lisbon International Airport

- Transportation: Lisbon has a passable public transit system, but it is not as good as in other European capitals. Reusable VivaViagem cards can be used on trams, buses, trains, and the metro and offer cheaper fares than single cost tickets. Additionally prevalent are taxis, tuk-tuks, and Uber..
- Money: Since it is a member of the EU and utilizes the Euro, Lisbon is a great place for travelers on a budget

because, in contrast to other European cities, your money goes a long way there. There are several ATMs, and most establishments accept credit cards. A quick sandwich costs less than 5 euros, a casual menu del día costs 8 euros, and sit-down meals start at 15 euros. Beer or a glass of wine costs as low as 2 euros.

- Weather: Lisbon experiences generally mild weather, with warm summers and cooler, rainier winters. While daytime temperatures in December and February average around 55 degrees F (13 degrees C), maximum temperatures in June and August often range from 80 to 90 degrees F (25 to 30 degrees C), but they are typically wetter than other times of the year. Sunny days and temperatures in the 70s F are typical during the beautiful spring and fall seasons (22-26 degrees C).
- Accommodation: Lisbon offers a variety of lodging options, from luxury hotels to affordable inns. Apartment rentals are a growingly popular choice, but because Lisbon is such a popular tourism destination, many apartment owners choose to rent through short-term websites like Airbnb rather than the more conventional long-term rental. Unfortunately, as a result, many inhabitants have moved outside of Lisbon's downtown.
- Lisbon Hills: Lisbon, like Rome, has seven hills, so no matter which way you walk, it feels like you are always going up. The inhabitants of Lisbon have devised a few simpler ways to get around these steep hills, including their famous trams and even an elevator in the midst of the city (I'll have more on these moments). I am more than delighted to hike these hills, mostly so I can justify eating all the pastel de nata.

TOURIST GIMMICKS.

- If I could give you one piece of advice, it would be this: walking is the best way to explore Lisbon!
- You'll feel perfectly at home in Lisbon if you prefer ambling along cobblestone streets, sitting outside on a cafe terrace to people-watch, or just purposefully getting lost.
- Don't let lists of things to do in Lisbon, like the one I'll offer below, trick you into thinking you must check off every item on the list. My favorite aspect of the city is how wonderful little details can be found all over.
- You never know what you'll find around the next corner: perhaps some vibrant, traditionally tiled buildings, an oddball craft store, a breathtaking view of the river Tejo, or even some amazing street art.
- Knowing that Lisbon has many hills is a beneficial thing. My legs were killing me from the first trip to Lisbon! Please bring some supportive walking shoes.
- Fortunately, public transportation in Lisbon is relatively affordable, and taxis and hailed trips are as well, allowing you to travel farther. It will cost between €5 and €7 to get from one side of the center to the other.

You won't have a bad time because Lisbon is a really safe and laid-back city.

There are, however, a few things you should be aware of before you go.

- First off, keep in mind that you are not at all in Spain. A very different language from Spanish is Portuguese. Use English instead of Spanish because this will make people dislike you. English is by far the most popular language to use and is widely spoken.
- Be aware that any bread, olives, or other side dishes that the restaurant serves on your table are not free

tapas. You must pay for them if you touch them. They're typically expensive! This is simply how things operate in Portugal; it's not a scam in any way.

- Some visitors are astonished to see drug traffickers in Rossio Square or Praça do Comércio. The majority of these men are genuine tourist scammers. They're inconvenient but not harmful; just tell them no thanks or ignore them, and they'll stop. Only contact them if you are in immediate need of oregano or baking powder.
- Use a ride-hailing app like Uber or Bolt, or learn what a cab will actually cost you. Unfortunately, some taxi drivers con uninformed tourists into overpaying. During a recent visit from my Dutch relatives, they spent 30 euros on a taxi from the airport that should have only cost them 7. Some prices in Lisbon may come as a shock to those from northern Europe.

Finally, there are a few attractions that, at this time, I would describe as tourist traps. Most significantly, you don't actually need to take Tram 28. Queuing takes forever, and the residents genuinely depend on that tram to go anywhere, so it's probably not worth your time. Belém Tower is also rather uninteresting. There is hardly much to see inside, despite the lengthy lines.

PACKING ESSENTIALS FOR A TRIP TO LISBON

Are you anticipating a trip to Lisbon and want to prepare by packing appropriately? Here are some of the greatest items to carry in your suitcase so that you'll be prepared for any excursion, from beachcombing to climbing, five-star resorts to remote getaways.

Basic Styling Advice

- Locals in Lisbon dress in a stylish, laid-back, and subtle elegance.

- Choose a stylish, casual outfit with beautiful shoes.
- Even if they are particularly popular among younger people, jeans are always classy and presentable.
- Make sure you bring comfortable daytime footwear because there will be a lot to see and a lot of walking to do (hotter shoes are good).
- Wear a sunhat and lots of sunscreen during the summer.
- Always have a pair of sunglasses with you because the sun can be bright at any time of year.
- There is a beach, but leave your swimming gear at home unless you are certain you will swim there or you are staying at a hotel with a pool.

Clothing Advice for Women

- In our opinion, save your shorts and sarongs for the beach; wearing them anywhere in the city will mark you as a tourist, and wearing skimpy, form-fitting clothing may draw unwelcome attention.
- We advise you to bring some wonderful glittering sandals and a nicer outfit for more upscale eateries.
- Take your heels, but save them for nightlife activities like clubbing or dinner.
- A pashmina is a stylish accessory that can be added to any ensemble.
- Be sure to cover your shoulders and bare legs if you want to visit any religious locations; a pashmina can help with this.

Dressing Advice for Men

- There are no particular points to draw your attention aside from going for a smart-casual style.
- We adore the SCOTTeVEST line of fantastic, multifunctional travel coats with numerous pockets and RFID security features.

- Commodious Attire That Is Simple To Dress Up Or Down.

Although the Portuguese want to look great, most of them prefer to be comfortable over having an overly dazzling appearance. Their style can be best described as casual elegant. If you want to be prepared for anything, including fine dining at a luxury resort in the Algarve, a wine tasting at a vineyard estate in the Alentejo, and even sightseeing in Lisbon, pack a variety of fancy and casual outfits and items that will go well together.

- Sunscreen

This is especially crucial in Lisbon and the Algarve, which are frequently mentioned as some of Europe's sunniest locations. In fact, considering the moderate year-round climate and the frequent occurrence of bright, sunny days in winter, sunscreen is among the most crucial items you can bring with you to Portugal. Of course, you should preserve your skin when you go to the beach, but you should also apply lotion to your face when you are in the cities and towns.

- Hiking sandals

In Portugal, walking is a necessity, so be ready for both the slick cobblestones and the sandy boardwalks. If you plan to hike up the mountainous streets of Lisbon, along the coast, or on the country's dirt roads, pack a pair of sturdy, comfortable shoes that look stylish, keep your feet cool, and protect you.

- A Windbreaker With A Built-In Raincoat (Especially During Late Fall Or Winter)

Those Atlantic winds have the power to swiftly turn a warm night cold. Why not bring one coat that acts as both a raincoat and raingear when traveling in the late fall, winter, and early spring?

- Swimwear

Portugal's most appealing features are, without a doubt, its stunning beaches and captivating coastline. What you carry will depend on the experience you're hoping for, from sunbathing to snorkeling. Considerable one-pieces, attractive bikinis, and rash guards are all worth considering. A 1-3 millimeter (0.03-0.11 inch) wet suit may be the best option if you're planning a surfing trip, even in the summer (the coast along the mainland has a reputation for being cold).

- A Bag With A Reliable Closure

Pickpockets should always be avoided when traveling. Portugal is generally a secure country, but popular locations like downtown Lisbon might draw pickpockets searching for unobservant tourists.

- Electric Adapter And Transformer

Bring an adaptor because you'll need to plug in your camera batteries, cell phones, e-readers, computers, and even hair styling tools. Portugal is comparable to many European nations in that it uses a standard voltage and frequency of 220 V and 50 Hz. It may be recommended to bring a transformer if you are traveling from a country like the United States, especially if you intend to use a hair dryer or curling/straightening iron because using an adaptor alone can cause the electricity to blow out and/or damage your device.

BUDGETING

It's common knowledge that Lisbon is the place to be these days. This city truly has it all with its classic architecture, breathtaking views, legendary cuisine, and never-ending nightlife. The massive increase in tourists—and subsequent increase in prices—can, however, be more of a curse than a blessing if you're traveling on a tight budget.

Even so, Lisbon can be a very reasonable city while still providing enough luxury for those who choose it. All you need to do is plan your trip carefully, steer clear of tourist traps, and seek out local favorites. In this travel guide, we'll tell you where to stay, what to do, and how to make the most of Lisbon on a budget.

The Most Economical Season to Visit Lisbon

- As with any popular vacation spot, Lisbon is best visited during the "shoulder" or low season (the months between low and high season). Less people, more options, and cheaper pricing result from this.
- The streets are crowded with tourists during the peak months of July and August, when temperatures can reach the upper eighties or higher (over 30 degrees Celsius). Lisbon can still be enjoyed throughout the summer, but it can be a hot, exhausting, and expensive holiday.
- By visiting Lisbon during the off-peak season, you may avoid all of that. With warm weather and the lowest prices, the winter is a stunning time to visit the city. The best months to travel are May, June, or September. It's warm and bright enough to spend as much time outside as you can during these shoulder season months, and you can even consider taking a day excursion from Lisbon to one of the surrounding beaches. In addition to

saving money overall by avoiding the tourist rush, lodging costs are still rather affordable

Cheapest Places To Stay In Lisbon

Lisbon's Top Hostels

Hostels are one thing Lisbon has in plenty. Since there is a severe lack of demand in this area, each hostel must go above and beyond the call of duty to flourish. The competition to provide the finest experience at the lowest price is fantastic news for backpackers and budget travelers since you can't lose.

In Lisbon, some hostels are better than others. Home Lisbon Hostel, which is in the heart of Baixa, is one of our favorites. There are also reasonably priced private rooms available, and even the dorms feel more like hotel rooms here. The daily family supper is a great chance to meet other travelers and only costs €10 for a three-course home-cooked meal. Yes! In terms of quality, Lisbon Hostel and Sant Jordi Hostels Lisbon are also excellent choices.

Lisbon Top Hostels

Affordable Accommodations in Lisbon

There are several hotels in Lisbon that offer a little more solitude at totally affordable prices if you're not into the hostel lifestyle.

A Casa das Janelas com Vista offers comfortable accommodations, a sumptuous breakfast, and views of Bairro Alto (as the name implies). Or check out 1869 Prncipe Real, one of Lisbon's top boutique hotels. It's incredible that the amount of comfort, style, and individualized care offered here can be had for such an affordable price. At 54 Santa Catarina, you can even splash out on a luxurious penthouse with a terrace. Although it can cost a little more, the value for your money is almost as breathtaking as the view.

Walking the Streets

When it comes to entertaining on a shoestring budget, Lisbon is very much unsurpassed when it comes to Here, you don't have to spend a lot of money to have fun. You can pass hours just aimlessly exploring the streets. Discover Alfama's hills, ascend to the top of each miradouro, and stroll along the water to enjoy the sea wind. It's actually a blessing in disguise to get lost here because you never know what treasures you'll find.

Walking down Lisbon famous restaurant and store-lined street

Lisbon Offers Affordable Food You'll Actually Want to Eat

The last component of Portuguese culture that we love is cuisine! Although eating for free might be a stretch, Lisbon is the best city to sample fine dining on a budget. And fortunately for you, many of Lisbon's must-try dishes also happen to be among the least expensive.

The bifana is evidence that an excellent meal doesn't have to be elaborate or expensive. Credit for image: @anastasia.raykova

Avoid posh restaurants and opt for Lisbon's best street food bites for the most authentic dining experience. Don't forget:

Bifana is a tasty sandwich prepared with stewed pork.

P.O. with chouriço chorizo-stuffed bread

Pastéis de nata are custard-filled tarts made of puff pastry.

A cherry liqueur called ginjinha is served in little cups.

After you've had your fill of street food, visit one of Lisbon's top places for inexpensive eats, where you can eat like a king or queen for only a few euros. Some of our favorites include A Provinciana for the prato do dia, or plate of the day, served at lunchtime, and Zé da Mouraria (Rua Joo do Outeiro 24), where the quantities are designed for sharing.

CREATING AN ITINERARY

Lisbon is a magnificent city in and of itself, but there are a few worthwhile day trips that can be taken from Lisbon as well. Depending on how much time you have to travel outside the city and see those places, this may require you to stay an additional day or two.

The ideal length of time to spend in Lisbon is three days, which will give you enough time to both see the city and go on a day trip, which we recommend being to Sintra.

Although it can be completed in two days, we strongly advise skipping the day trip to Sintra and sticking to Lisbon. One day is a stretch, but Lisbon is a rather tight city, so you can visit SOME of the things and decide what you want to see more of on your return trip.

Let's now discuss how to spend your time in Lisbon specifically. We'll assume you have three full days to visit Lisbon, excluding your travel days, because we landed there late at night (arriving in Lisbon and leaving Lisbon).

Before we continue, a little remark about our travel preferences: we don't particularly enjoy visiting museums or exploring every single church in a city like Lisbon, where the Catholic population is still over 80%.

The reason you'll see a walking tour and a food tour on our agenda rather than a list of six cathedrals and three museums is that we're much more interested in activities that put us in touch with residents who can show us their interpretation of the city. I think different strokes for different people, I think, but we'd much rather spend our time exploring fewer things in depth than hopping from tourist attraction to tourist attraction in an effort to see everything.

If this is your first visit, you need at least a full weekend in Lisbon to see everything. You can experience the finest of Lisbon in 3 days without feeling rushed.

This sample schedule, which was based on my own 3-day trip to Lisbon, is ideal if this is your first time there.

- Day 1: Baixa, Chiado, and Alfama Walking Tour

Spend your first day in Lisbon exploring the city's main tourist district, which includes Baixa, Chiado, and Alfama, its most romantic and endearing neighborhood.

But First, Coffee

It's wonderful to hear that Lisbon has a surprisingly active specialty coffee scene. I adore coffee, and I particularly enjoy trying it in novel ways, whether it be in the form of a novel beverage, beans from a location I've never visited before, or novel flavors or preparation methods.

Being a bit of a coffee nerd, I set out to find Lisbon's best coffee during our visit there.

Here are the two locations that I'd suggest visiting that are close to Lisbon's center.

You may find roasters from Berlin, Barcelona, Amsterdam, and other locations even farther away at Bloom Coffee Room, where they handpick the best beans from all around Europe. We enjoyed the nicest coffee in Lisbon at this location.

Fábrica Coffee Roasters is expanding its empire of speciality coffee shops in Portugal and has several sites throughout the city (now they have a location in Porto, too). The cappuccino we got there was the greatest we'd had in Portugal since they roast their own beans.

- Day 1 morning—The Baixa neighborhood

The Baixa neighborhood is Lisbon's grand center, home to magnificent plazas and busy shopping streets. The district was entirely wrecked by the earthquake of 1755, and its restoration produced the first grid system in history. Today, Baixa is a lively and fascinating city that is a delight to visit and a great place to start your tour of Lisbon.

If not, take the metro to the Rossio or Terreiro do Paco metro stations. Baixa is Lisbon's primary tourist district, and you will likely be based nearby.

The Grand Praca do Comércio Plaza, which served as Lisbon's first commercial hub, is located on the southern side of Baixa and overlooks the Tejo Estuary. The Rua Augusta, which branches off of Praca do Comércio, is a charming retail district with outdoor cafes and an eclectic mix of independent stores and eateries.

Observation: Be sure to visit the spectacular vantage point at the top of the Arco da Rua Augusta.

The Elevador de Santa Justa, a lift with a neo-gothic design that takes passengers up one of Lisbon's steepest hills, is located along the Rua Augusta. Rossio Plaza, considered by Lisbon residents to be the city's beating heart, is located on the north side of Rua Augusta.

Beyond Rossio lies the square of the restaurateurs, home to the distinctive pink Foz Palace and an obelisk memorial. After a morning of touring, treat yourself to a glass of Ginjinha—a sweet cherry liqueur—at A Ginjinha bar, the neighborhood establishment known for its cocktails.

Rossio Square

Praco do Comercio

- Day 1 afternoon: The Alfama Neighborhood

It is advised that you visit the Alfama district's hills and charming streets in the afternoon. The oldest neighborhood in Lisbon, Alfama, provides a stark contrast to Baixa's opulence and regularity. The layout of the city is a maze of cobblestoned lanes and alleys that date back to the early medieval period. Alfama was formerly Lisbon's poorest neighborhood, yet it now exudes a fashionable, artisanal attitude while still taking pride in its history.

Many of Lisbon's oldest structures, including the Se Cathedral, Catelo de Sao Jorge, and Igreja de San António—a church devoted to Lisbon's patron saint—can be found in Alfama. The number 28 tram route, with its vibrant yellow trams, runs through the heart of Alfama.

A tour of the neighborhood might be strenuous due to the numerous high hills in Alfama. The Miradouro da Graca, the Portas dos Sol, or the view from the castle walls, are just a few of the breathtaking views that await those who climb to the summit of these hills.

Fado, a melancholy musical genre that was originally sung by sailors' wives while they awaited the return of their beloved sailors, has its roots in Alfama. You can watch live fado performances in a lot of the tiny eateries in the Alfama and Bairro Alto neighborhoods in the evenings.

Listed below are some ideas for things to do and see in Alfama.

The Castle of Saint Jorge Alfama sprawls from the walls of the castelo, which is perched atop the hill, and down the hill toward the river. Before the Portuguese captured Lisbon and made it their capital, it served as a crucial defensive position and the site of numerous fights over the centuries. It has served as many other things since then, including a hospital and a prison, and it wasn't until the 20th century that it was returned to its previous splendor. Today, you may pay 10 euros to enter the grounds and, most importantly, walk along the castle walls to take in the breathtaking views.

Sao Jorge castle

Alfama has a number of excellent vantage locations, including two that are only a few blocks apart from one another. The first is called Miradouro de Santa Luzia, and it offers a pleasant perspective of the river . On the side of the Igreja de Santa Luzia (near the lookout), there are some interesting tiles to check out that show a struggle for the Castelo. The Igreja of So Vicente de Fora, which is located on a hill to the northeast, is visible from Miradouro das Portas do Sol , which offers even better views of the river. The statue of St. Vincent, Lisbon's patron saint, should not be missed. The second vantage point features a charming little outside terrace with a bar, which would be a perfect place to enjoy, say, an Aperol Spritz or a Port Tonic while admiring the sun's golden glow lighting up the hillside.

Santa Luzia Viewpoint

Even if you don't think canned fish is for you, you should at least taste it once when visiting Lisbon. And in our opinion, this is the best location for it. She works hard to make sure her product is sustainable, from the fish to the cans, and she owns it. Her family has been in the fishing business for centuries. We tried a lot, but the bacalhau (cod) with garlic and olive oil was by far our favorite. If you're not a big fan of fish flavors, it was the least "fishy" option. You have a choice of purchasing some to eat at the quaint eatery or picking up some cans to consume later. They also make wonderful gifts to take back to friends and family.

28 Tram

Alfama streets

- Day Two: The Belem neighborhood

Belem is a charming city to the west of Lisbon that abuts the Tejo Estuary.

Vasco da Gama spent his final night at Belem, which historically housed Lisbon's shipyards, before embarking on his legendary journey to India. Later, the spectacular Mosteiro dos Jerónimos was built with the enormous wealth made from the 17th-century spice trade.

Belem, a charming neighborhood with parks, tree-lined plazas, and a beautiful riverbank stroll, is currently celebrating its seafaring heritage.

Observation: The E15 tram runs from Belem to the Baixa neighborhood in central Lisbon.

The impressive Padro dos Descobrimentos monument and the Torre de Belem fort, which historically protected the city from seaborne assaults, are located along Belem's picturesque waterfront.

Within a half-day of tourism, the majority of the city's tourist attractions can be viewed. Visitors typically stay longer, though, to enjoy the picturesque riverfront or explore one of the city's renowned museums, including the Colecáo Berardo art gallery, MAAT, or Museu Nacional dos Coches.

Padrao dos Descobrimentos

Torre de Belem

- LX Factory or a ride on the 28 tram on Day 2 in the afternoon.

It is advised to visit Lisbon's artisan district, the LX Factory, in the afternoon. This former factory is now home to a variety of interesting stores, eateries, oddball vendors, artist studios, and urban art exhibits.

Observation: LX Factory is well positioned to visit after Belem and is on the E15 tram route.

A different option in the afternoon is to take the number 28 tram along its picturesque route from Alfama and Baixa in the east to the

Estrela districts in the west. The 28 tram is a great way to see the city because it travels through several of Lisbon's historic districts.

Lx Factory shopping mall

- Day 2 evening: An evening spent at Bairro Alto and Cais do Sodré (Friday or Saturday).

Lisbon's Bairro Alto and Pink Street are Lisbon's two primary nightlife districts (in Cais do Sodre).

The maze-like neighborhood of Bairro Alto is home to a variety of fado music establishments and numerous bars. On weekends, the neighborhood transforms into one big party as people socialize in the streets.

Around 2 a.m., the pubs in Bairro Alto close, but in the Cais do Sodre neighborhood, the excitement never ends. Originally a red-light area, Cais do Sodro is now the center of Lisbon's nightlife, with many of the clubs located along Pink Street.

Lisbon's Pink Street

- Day three: Bairro Alto and Principe Real in the morning.

Enjoy a stroll around Bairro Alto, Principe Real, and Avenida da Liberdade, three of Lisbon's most attractive neighborhoods, in the morning of the third day.

The center of Lisbon's nightlife is Bairro Alto, and chances are you've already seen some of the neighborhoods at night. But during the day, you may explore the crowded Praca Luis de Camóes plaza, the Convento do Carmo ruins, and the lovely Igreja de Sáo Roque interior.

Prncipe Real is a wealthy neighborhood with opulent 20th-century structures and a decidedly Portuguese vibe. This is most likely due to the neighborhoods in Lisbon that are the most truly Portuguese that you will see during your three days there. The Jardim do Principe Real is located in the middle of the Prince Real, and the magnificent Miradouro de Sao Pedro de Alcántra viewpoint lies on the eastern side.

Lisbon's most upscale shopping district, the Avenida da Liberdade, is home to numerous designer stores and distinctive boutiques. Even if you aren't in the area to shop, this broad boulevard is a delightful spot to wander because it is bordered by trees and formal gardens. The Praca Marques de Pombal and the Parque Eduardo VII are located at the top of Avenida da Liberdade

Pricipe Real

- Day 3 afternoon in Lisbon: Parque das Nacóes

The ultra-modern Lisbon neighborhood known as Parque das Nacóes was built in preparation for Expo '98. Along with exhibits and gardens created specifically for the Expo, the area is dotted with impressive modernist architecture.

On a bright day, Parque das Nacoes in Lisbon is a great place to go because it has wide areas, riverfront walks, and a tranquil environment.

One of Europe's greatest aquariums, the beautiful Oceanário de Lisboa, is the main draw for tourists. In addition to Torre Vasco da Gama, Lisbon's tallest structure, a cable car, a casino, a contemporary shopping mall, and a variety of restaurants are also located in the vicinity.

The Torre Vasco da Gama, parque das nacóes

CHAPTER TWO
ENJOY LISBON ALL YEAR

ANNUAL FESTIVAL AND EVENTS

Lisbon hosts a variety of entertaining events and festivals throughout the year, and you can enjoy them if you know what activities are scheduled for each month.

While this is happening, there are activities happening all around Lisbon, but especially in the Graça, Mouraria, Bica, and Alfama neighborhoods, where throngs enjoy street parties (arraiais), dances, music, and lots of beer and sardines! The party doesn't end on Saint Anthony's Day; throughout the entire month of June, numerous cultural events, street concerts, and street parties bring the city to life. Meanwhile, the pubs and clubs are continually packed. The Lisbon Festival brings the entire city out onto the streets, making it the ideal opportunity to get to know the locals and experience daily life in the riverside white city!

New Year's Concert in January

On January 1, Centro Cultural de Belém (CCB) and the Lisbon Metropolitan Orchestra host a customary concert to ring in the new year. Tickets cost between $5 and €18.

New year eve 2022 Lisbon

The Teatro Nacional de So Carlos will host a concert of classical music by the Portuguese Symphonic Orchestra on January 3 as part of its New Year's Concert series.

Even though January 6 is not a holiday in Portugal, it is celebrated by eating the customary Bolo Rei (King's Cake), also known as Epiphany or Three Kings' Day (Dia do Reis in Portuguese).

February's Carnival

Around Lisbon, particularly in Torres Vedras and Sesimbra, there are carnival parades and celebrations that feature Brazilian-inspired costumes and samba music. Lisbon nightclubs that host costume ball events

Lisbon is the ideal location to wow your special someone. What could be more romantic on February 14th than to choose the ideal romantic hotel and choose a rooftop restaurant in Lisbon with breathtaking views of the cityscape and the River Tejo?

In less than an hour from Lisbon, in the Mardi Gras parades, Brazilian costumes and samba music fill the streets of Torres Vedras and the tourist town of Sesimbra. Carnival celebrations are also hosted by a few bars and clubs in Lisbon.

March

Lisbon March Meia Marathon

The half-marathon in Lisbon is a wonderful opportunity to cross the 25 de Abril Bridge over the River Tejo and take in the magnificence of Lisbon's cityscape. The Jerónimos Monastery, a Unesco World Heritage Site, serves as the finish line for the Meia Maratona.

Lisbon Fashion Week's Moda Lisboa showcases the newest collections from Portuguese designers.

Lisbon Half Marathon: A wonderful chance to stroll across Lisbon's Tejo River Bridge and take in the beauty of the town.

Monstra: Attend the animated film festival in Lisbon to see some of the best cartoons ever made.

The clocks advance by one hour at the stroke of midnight on the last Sunday in March to mark the start of daylight saving time

April

Indie Lisbon, April

An independent, 11-day film festival called Indie Lisboa showcases experimental, documentary, and short films from all genres, both in Portugal and abroad. A parallel events schedule features discussions, panel discussions, and unique activities with movie producers, programmers, distributors, critics, and other industry professionals.

Fish in Lisbon.

Fish in Lisbon, also known as Peixe em Lisboa, is an annual celebration for people who enjoy seafood. Try our freshest fish and seafood prepared in a variety of ways by the most creative chefs and restaurants from Portugal and around the world. In Pavilho Carlos Lopes' Eduardo VII Park, the event is held.

Dialects of Music

The Centro Cultural de Belém (CCB) hosts Music Days, a three-day nonstop music festival, in the spring. Concerts of jazz, opera, and classical music, workshops, and other activities are all part of the program.

25 April: a big march down Avenida da Liberdade from Marquês do Pombal Square to the Rossio, as well as additional celebrations taking place all around the city, commemorating the national holiday honoring the nonviolent Revolution of 1974. The Carnation Revolution, as it is often known, was led by the military and ended Portugal's 40-year dictatorship while granting independence to former Portuguese colonies.

Tennis fans may choose to attend the Estoril Open to watch their favorite players in action. Estoril, where the competition is held, is just two stations away from Cascais train station.

May

Workers' Day: Portugal observes a national holiday on the first of May. The two major Portuguese trade unions typically organize parades and protests at Alameda D. Afonso Henriques (CGTP) and Belém Tower to mark the occasion (UGT).

Documentaries, shorts, and experimental films of many genres are shown at the independent Indie Lisboa festival, which runs for 11 days.

Lisbon Under the Stars: An immersive production that combines visual effects with computer-generated performers and musicians. The ruins of Carmo Convent serve as the starting point of an online tour through 600 years of Portuguese history.

Enjoy jazz, soul, funk, and hip-hop music every Sunday from May to September at the Out Jazz Festival in Lisbon's public gardens. The concerts this month begin at 5 p.m. in the grounds near to Belém Tower. Free entry is offered.

Out jazz 2022

An event that is expected to have an impact on the Portuguese contemporary art industry is the international contemporary art fair, ARCO Lisboa, which brings together up-and-coming and established artists.

June

The most significant annual event in Lisbon is the Feast of Saint Anthony, which is observed on the evening of June 12 but is actually a month-long celebration with numerous events and activities taking place all throughout the city.

The Lisbon Book Fair is held annually in Eduardo VII Park in the first half of June. Despite the fact that most books are in Portuguese, it offers a chance to experience Lisbon's public park and its inhabitants. Mon–Thu 12:30–11:00, Fri 12:30–0:00, Sat 11:00–0:00, and Sunday and holidays 11:01–11:00.

Lisbon Under the Stars: an immersive production that combines visual effects with computer-generated performers and musicians. For the entire month of May and the first half of June, Carmo Convent's Ruins serve as the backdrop for a virtual trip through 600 years of Portuguese history.

Enjoy jazz, soul, funk, and hip-hop music every Sunday from May to September at the Out Jazz Festival in Lisbon's public gardens. The concerts this month begin at 5 p.m. in Campo Grande Garden. Free entry is offered.

Out jazz festival Lisbon

July

Festival ao Largo: The Teatro Nacional de So Carlos, Lisbon's Opera House, hosts free outdoor classical music concerts, opera, ballet, and dance productions.

NOS Alive is a three-day music event that takes place in Passeio Martimo de Algés, not far from Belém. The UK publication NME named the festival as one of the top 12 festivals in Europe.

Super Bock Super Rock is a 3-day music festival with many well-known bands from throughout the world, plenty of sunshine, and beer. Just 10 minutes from Sesimbra's Meco beach is where Super Bock Super Rock is held. The estate is called Herdade do Cabeço da Flauta. Lisbon is only a one-hour drive from the festival.

EDP Cool Jazz is not technically a summer festival; rather, it is a series of events featuring a variety of genres inspired by jazz, held in Cascais, a coastal resort 30 minutes from Lisbon. Jamie Cullum, Diana Krall, and Tom Jones are the featured performers this year. The performances last the entire month of July.

Free live theater productions and music concerts energize the Baixa neighborhood. On the weekends from July to September, visit Rua Augusta to see the street art.

Enjoy jazz, soul, funk, and hip-hop music every Sunday from May to September at the Out Jazz Festival in Lisbon's public gardens. The concerts this month begin at 5 p.m. in Jardim da Estrela. Free entry is offered.

August

Jazz em Agosto, Lisbon's premier annual jazz festival, is held in August at the Gulbenkian Foundation and features concerts by internationally renowned artists in an outdoor amphitheatre. To supplement the program, there are free concerts.

The Jardim das Oliveiras park at CCB, Belém will host jazz and world music performances as well as movie screenings this summer. Throughout August, there are outdoor movie showings on Fridays at 9.30 p.m. and musical performances at 7 p.m. on Saturdays and Sundays. Entry is uncharged.

Enjoy jazz, soul, funk, and hip-hop music every Sunday in Lisbon's public gardens from May to September as part of the Out Jazz Festival. The concerts this month begin at 5 p.m. in Terreiro do Paço's Ribeira das Naus neighborhood. Entry is uncharged.

September

From now through the end of September, Com'Out Lisbon is offering free performances of fado, jazz, magic, theater, and dance.

The Lisbon International Horror Film Festival is a must-attend event for lovers of the genre.

Santa Casa Alfama's Fado Festival is a two-day opportunity to hear some of the top fado singers currently performing and to experience true Portuguese culture.

Enjoy jazz, soul, funk, and hip-hop music every Sunday from May to September at the Out Jazz Festival in Lisbon's public gardens. The concerts this month begin at 5 p.m. at Parque da Bela Vista. Free entry is offered.

October

The Lisbon Marathon: Starting in Cascais and covering 42 kilometers (26 miles) to the finish line in Lisbon, the marathon offers breathtaking views the entire way. Two shorter distance races are part of the event: the Luso Half Marathon, which spans the Vasco da Gama Bridge, one of the longest in Europe; and the Vodafone 10K, formerly known as the Vodafone Mini Marathon, which spans the 25 de Abril Bridge.

Portugal's newest collections are shown at Europe's oldest independent fashion week, Moda Lisboa.

Lisbon fashion week

A festival promoting French cinema is held each year in Lisbon in October. It is sponsored by the French Embassy and the Portuguese Cinematheque.

Another film festival that takes place in Lisbon is called DocLisboa, and it is dedicated solely to documentaries. The top contemporary documentaries produced by renowned world filmmakers are shown throughout this 11-day festival.

Although the days are still rather long this month, the clocks will be turned back one hour at 2 a.m. on October 31. This will cause dusk to occur much earlier.

November

Web Summit is the tech event that is the buzz of the town, drawing 70,000 attendees to Lisbon.

The Film Festival of Lisbon and Sintra (LEFFEST): This yearly event features cinema screenings, conferences, readings, master courses, performances, and exhibitions in both Lisbon and the picturesque resort of Sintra.

Super Bock im Stock is an autumn music festival that takes place on November 23–24. It has outstanding musicians from various genres, including jazz, funk, rock, pop, electronic, and indie music. On Avenida da Liberdade, the street that runs through downtown Lisbon's Baixa, the festival is held in theaters, churches, and even the Rossio train station.

December

There are many Christmas markets in Lisbon, including the Rossio Christmas Market and the one at Praça do Municpio (both in the Baixa, Lisbon's central business district). These Christmas markets are great for picking up gifts, and they often feature live cooking demonstrations, music, and kid-friendly entertainment.

Predominantly sacred music is performed by churches throughout Lisbon.

The Corrida So Silvestre de Lisboa: The 10-kilometer city race is a well-attended event. The river and Lisbon's main streets are still gleaming with Christmas lights as runners cross the finish line and start their journey in Praça dos Restauradores. It occurs at 5.30 p.m. on the final Saturday of each year. required to register and pay a charge.

Here are some fantastic New Year's Eve activities, including a free fireworks display in Terreiro do Paço, romantic meals, fado performances, and river cruises.

LISBON'S SEASONAL ACTIVITIES

While on vacation in Lisbon, one can participate in a number of seasonal activities. Lisbon seems to be nice in the summer, yet many people prefer to travel there in the winter and some others in the fall or spring. Here are some seasonal activities that one might enjoy.

SUMMER

Are you a new visitor wondering what to do in Lisbon, Portugal, during the summer? Continue reading for inspiring ideas that will have you wanting to pack your bags right away!

The Top 10 Lisbon Activities

- Go surfing.
- Investigate Praça do Comércio
- Rossio Plaza (Pedro IV Square)
- The Tower of Belem (Torre de Belem)
- At the Monastery of Jeronimo at Panteao National

- ➢ Take Tram 28 for a trip.
- ➢ Spend the day at Sintra.
- ➢ Ascend the Santa Justa Elevator.
- ➢ Take some time to explore Cascais.

#1. Go surfing

Did you know that Portugal is one of Europe's top destinations for surfing? Because Lisbon is located directly on the Atlantic and boasts enormous waves that draw surfers from all over the world, surfing is one of the best activities to do in Lisbon.

There are several surf locations near Lisbon's city center, and some of them even feature different sorts of waves that last all year (which makes it an ideal place to reside for surfing vacations). The well-known beaches of Ericeira, Alentejo, Cascais, and other locations are among the best to visit for surfing.

#2. Investigate Praca do Comercio.

Lisbon in the summer is magical and there are lots of interesting things to see, aside from the sparkling waters and ferocious waves. The Praça do Comércio, for instance, is one of Lisbon's top attractions and is unquestionably worth a trip if you're in the area. An 18th-century square with stunning historic buildings and statues is encircled by hip stores and eateries.

#3. Rossio Plaza (Pedro IV Square).

You should also visit Rossio Square, which is considered to be Lisbon's most renowned square. What was formerly a location for public executions in the 16th century is today a fantastic meeting place for both locals and visitors.

#4. The Tower of Belem (Torre de Belem).

A must-see landmark on the Tagus River is Belem Tower. When this stunning tower was first constructed in 1515, it was used by Lisbon to defend itself from seaborne attackers.

#5. At the Monastery of Jeronimo at Panteao.

Panteao Nacional is a baroque 16th-century church that was later turned into Lisbon's National Pantheon. This beautiful church is a part of Lisbon's iconic skyline, and it also offers a fantastic overlooking view of the city when you climb up to the top of the Dom.

Another fun summer activity in Lisbon is a visit to Jeronimo's Monastery. The Jeronimo Monastery, which was built in 1504 and is located in the western section of the city, boasts exceptional architecture and a fascinating history. This structure represented Portugal's wealth and power during the Age of Discovery. It is now regarded as one of the major tourist attractions in Lisbon.

#5. Take Tram 28 For A Trip.

Taking a ride on Lisbon's renowned Tram 28 is another must-do activity. As is well known, Lisbon's trams are unquestionably national symbols, and Tram 28 is among the most visited sights in the city. You shouldn't pass up the chance to take this tram if you want to tour Lisbon's historic districts without having to do any walking.

#6. Spend The Day At Sintra.

You must go to the area of Sintra if you love distinctive and colorful architecture. Although Sintra is not located in Lisbon, you may travel there swiftly by car or train. The gorgeous palaces of Sintra, such as the Pena Palace and Monserrate Palace, are renowned for their colorful beauty and stand out magnificently from the hilltops. There are no vistas like those in Sintra!

#7. Ascend The Santa Justa Elevador.

The Elevador de Santa Justa is one of Lisbon's most distinctive views. The original purpose of this Neo-Gothic building was for public transportation to and from the Baixa and Bairro Alto neighborhoods. Since then, many visitors now consider it a must-see. From the top platform of the lift, which ascends seven stories along a steep hill, you can see an amazing view of Lisbon.

#8. Take Some Time To Explore Caiscas.

If you're thinking about visiting Lisbon, you should also think about going to its breathtaking neighbor, Cascais. With a 3€ train ticket, you can go to Cascais from the heart of Lisbon in about 30 minutes. Cascais is the ideal day excursion from Lisbon with a bustling holiday feel thanks to its stately structures, opulent houses, breathtaking cliff landscape, and beaches at virtually every corner.

Lisbon in the summer is the ideal destination for a vacation. You'll never run out of things to do in Lisbon, Portugal, with its clear skies, warm climate, and intriguing attractions.

WINTER

Consider going to Lisbon during the colder months. It's a fantastic plan! Lisbon is most popular during the summer, although it's very pleasant in the winter. In comparison to other European cities, the weather is excellent, there are fewer tourists than normal, and prices are lower. You understand, you'll like visiting Lisbon off-peak! What should one do there? Check out this list of wintertime activities in Lisbon!

#1.Visit The Oldest Running Bookstore In The World.

Livraria Bertrand's actual inauguration date is a little hazy; it was initially founded in 1732 but relocated to its current location following the Lisbon earthquake in 1755. However, one thing is certain: the library is very old. It has even received recognition from the dependable Guinness World Records team.

There are now multiple Bertrand stores in Lisbon, so be sure to choose the correct one (it's in Chiado) so you may discover the city's literary heritage and see rooms devoted to significant authors from the previous three centuries. Who doesn't enjoy the cozy atmosphere of a bookstore in the winter too?

#2. The Super Bock 'Em Stock Features Live Music.

We love music festivals, as you may have guessed. And it so happens that Lisbon is the location of a ton of our favorites all year long. In a variety of locations throughout the city, Super Bock im Stock presents exciting and eclectic alternative music talent during the winter months, namely on the 23–24 of November.

This time, the iconic Johnny Marr heads the program, which also includes performances over the weekend by Jungle, Rejjie Snow, U.S. Girls, Capito Fausto, and Masego, among a host of other enthralling up-and-coming artists.

#3. Visit The Calouste Gulbenkian Museum To Learn Something New.

The exhibition Art and Architecture between Lisbon and Baghdad, which is on display from October 26 through January 28, provides a fascinating look at the modernization of Baghdad, the capital of Iraq, during the 1960s and the part the Portuguese Calouste Gulbenkian Foundation played in this development and cultural exchange. On particular occasions, there will also be a number of seminars and conversations on the subject. Of course, all of this is in addition to the museum's outstanding permanent collection.

#4. Port Wine

Yes, I am aware that strictly speaking, this one is more appropriate for Porto than Lisbon, but the city offers a wide variety of opportunities to sample some of the most distinctively Portuguese alcoholic beverages. If there is a better season to drink fortified wine than in the winter, I haven't found it yet (and I've done some pretty extensive research). It's one of the best inventions that humans have ever made.

You can't really beat Solar do Vinho do Porto in terms of selection and history, though some people have complained that the service is a touch lacking. You may also check out what Chafariz do Vinho has to offer. And although a vintage bottle might cost quite a bit, a great glass doesn't necessarily require breaking the bank.

#5. Consume Pastés

Anyone who has even a passing familiarity with the city is aware of Pastéis de Belém and its signature treats. By almost all accounts, the renowned Lisbon restaurant is the best place in the world to find the famous custard tarts.

However, in recent years, some individuals have begun to assert that the pastéis from Manteigaria are actually superior, so you can consider visiting there to compare and decide for yourself. But Belém is unrivaled in terms of history and tradition.

Similar to port, these can be enjoyed at any time of the year, but there is something particularly alluring about downing a few glasses and munching on some sweets during the winter.

CHAPTER THREE BEST ATTRACTIONS, STREETS, ANDCITY SECRETS.

LISBON, PORTUGAL'S MUST-SEE ATTRACTIONS

Lisbon, which is spread out over seven hills and the Tagus River, is home to a striking Moorish castle, whimsical Manueline buildings that hint at the Age of Discovery, and antique trams that rattle from one famous site, gallery, and hilltop vantage point to the next. Are you staying past the weekend? Additionally, you'll have time to take day trips to Sintra's castles and palaces or the modern Parque das Naçes neighborhood, where one of the continent's most breathtaking aquariums is located.

- São Jorge Castle

Building, Museum

Lisbon's stronghold, which sits atop a hill above the old city, transports you back in time. A community has existed here since the 7th century BCE, according to the archaeological site, but it dates to the 11th century, when the city was ruled by the Moors. You may play "identify the landmark" here or climb the ramparts for sweeping views from the pine-shaded ramparts, a glance through the camera obscura, and a dose of history at the museum.

- Carmo Convent

Ruins

As you stroll through Lisbon's upscale Chiado neighborhood, you notice the mysterious ruins of this medieval convent, which have the arches and pillars of its nave open to the sky. It was destroyed by the 1755 earthquake and rebuilt in 1389 as a convent for the Carmelite order. In its archaeological museum, you may see prehistoric artifacts, Moorish friezes, and pre-Columbian ceramics alongside a church that is exquisitely tiled with Baroque azulejos (glazed, ornamental tiles).

- Sé Cathedral

Cathedral, Church, Mosque

In front of Lisbon's fortified cathedral, one of the city's most recognizable landmarks, vintage tram 28E comes to a stop. After the city was retaken from the invading Moors, Afonso I, Portugal's first monarch, erected it high and strong over the ruins of a mosque. Make sure to spend some time studying the Roman and Arabic archaeological remains in the cloisters after seeing the gothic arches and medieval statues in the vaulted interior.

- The National Azulejo Museum

Museum, Art Gallery

Take bus 759 to travel to this meticulously restored 16th-century Manueline convent, which is located just east of town and is known for its history and artistic azulejos. From the Renaissance to the Baroque and Contemporary, the collection is a wonderful journey through 500 years of azulejo craftsmanship. Visit the magnificently tiled former refectory for coffee.

➢ Cristo Rei Monument

Memorial, Park

The Cristo Rei monument is really located in Almada, which is only across the Tagus River from Lisbon. It has religious significance in the nation and was constructed under Salazar to imitate Rio de Janeiro's Christ the Redeemer statue.

- The National Museum of Ancient Art

Art Gallery, Museum

One of Lisbon's most stunning collections of ancient art is housed in this museum, which is located in a baroque palace just a short distance west of the city. The artifacts include sculpture from Egypt and Rome; ancient master paintings; Portuguese goldwork from the Age of Discovery; as well as priceless linens, lacquered furniture, and Asian pottery. The St. Jerome in His Study (1521) by Renaissance master Albrecht Dürer and the St. Vincent Panels (1460) by Nuno Gonçalves are not to be missed

➢ Building of the Lisbon Oceanarium Aquarium

This huge aquarium, which serves as the focal point of Lisbon's cutting-edge Parque das Naçes neighborhood, is Europe's biggest and, possibly, its best at simulating the terrestrial and marine ecosystems of the planet. Huge tanks are filled with puffins, penguins, jellyfish, sunfish, stingrays, and playful sea otters. You can even spend the night with sharks if you so choose.

- The Berardo Museum

This gallery is Lisbon's go-to for modern and contemporary art and is without a doubt the center of attention at the Belém Cultural Center. It displays works from billionaire José Berardo's collection, which ranges from kinetic and pop art to abstract, surrealist, and expressionist pieces. The paintings by artists like Warhol, Pollock, Man Ray, Dali, and Picasso, as well as the sculptures by Antony Gormley and Henry Moore, are given top priority. Visit on Saturday when admission is free to save money.

- Belém Tower

Due to its function in defending Portugal's coast during the Age of Discoveries and subsequently, Belém Tower is another Unesco World Heritage Site. The Belém Tower, which resembles the Jerónimos Monastery and has a similar blend of Gothic and Manueline design, draws tourists because of both its aesthetic appeal and historical significance. The entrance fee is €6 (£5.50).

Miradouro Senhora do Monte

Miradouro da Graça

- Miradouros

The challenging ascent to Lisbon's miradouros (lookouts) is worthwhile for the breathtaking panoramas that await. Some even offer outdoor cafés where you can relax while taking in the scenery. Favorite views include those of the Ponte 25 de Abril suspension bridge loping across the river, the Miradouro da Graça, and the highest of the high, Miradouro Senhora do Monte, which looks out over terracotta rooftops to the So Jorge Castle. It feels more bohemian in the Miradouro de Santa Catarina, which is shaded by trees.

THE MAGNIFICENT STREETS OF LISBON

Lisbon is undoubtedly growing in popularity as a tourist destination and is drawing in Portuguese from all across the country. Being a flexible city, it offers a variety of locations to explore and several things to do to enjoy the city.

Lisbon can only be fully experienced by getting out and engaging all five senses. Some of the world's most gorgeous streets can be found in the Portuguese capital. Take a break from your schoolwork and go see them in person. You are given a list to help you write your script.

- ➢ Avenida da Liberdade Street

One of the principal thoroughfares in the Portuguese city, Avenida da Liberdade, joins Praça dos Restauradores with Praça do Marquês de Pombal. You simply need to walk a short distance if you are living in a student apartment in this district of Lisbon to fall in love with it.

Beautiful examples of 19th-century classical Portuguese architecture may be seen for almost two kilometers, and the two center squares have impressive statues and attractive fountains. Along the avenue, you will find a ton of fashionable shops as well as some great places to eat.

- ➢ Rua Augusta Street

Anyone visiting Lisbon must go to Rua Augusta. It is the major pedestrian street in the city and features a variety of businesses;

cafes with stunning terraces; mosaic tiles throughout the floors; and a truly lively and welcoming environment.

The famous Arco da Rua Augusta can be seen from the top of Rua Augusta, and if you walk a little farther, you can locate an elevator that will take you to the observation deck at the top of the arch. It is no doubt a location not to be missed!

➢ Rua Cor de Rosa Street

bar

The most "instagrammable" street in Lisbon is without a doubt Rua Cor de Rosa in Cais do Sodré. Along with a stunning pink tarmac on this street, also known as Rua Nova do Carvalho, you may stop by a few cafes and pubs to unwind during the day or night.

This is one of the busiest areas for nightlife in Lisbon. Furthermore, it has become a stepping stone due to its previous renown. The street was infamous for being a meeting point for local prostitutes and criminals, but now it's just a fun area to hang out with friends and, of course, snap gorgeous photos.

- Rua da Bica Street

Unquestionably, one of the attractions of Lisbon is Duarte Belo's Rua da Bica. It is one of the city's most popular photo locations, and as soon as you arrive, you'll notice the vibrant colors, the tram, the vibrant history, and the breathtaking view of the Tagus.

This well-known avenue, along with the Champs-Élysées in Paris and 5th Avenue in New York, was selected as the most beautiful streets in the world in 2017. The vote, which was conducted on multiple American websites, was based on the opinions and travel experiences of thousands of tourists in each location. One of the primary landmarks of the street, Elevador da Bica, which carries hundreds of tourists through this neighborhood of Lisbon each day, is this well-known funicular.

➢ Calçada de Santana Street

In the center of Lisbon, near the Torel viewpoint, lies the Santana walkway. It's a charming, steep, historic, and narrow street. The fado diva Amália Rodrigues was born at door number 2, and the everlasting poet Lus de Cames passed away here. This sidewalk's balcony number 198, which is bordered by lions, a sign of strength and power, also stands out.

The detour to Calçada Nova do Colégio and Rua Martim Vaz, from where you can enter the Santos courtyard, are also on this itinerary. If you keep walking, you will soon arrive at the Hospital de San José. The Igreja da Pena, one of the city's original churches, is also located on this street, and you can still see the lovely Tagus in the background.

LISBON

DISCOVER LOCAL TREASURES

Go off-the-beaten-path whenever you want to in Lisbon. Go off-the-beaten-path whenever you want to in Lisbon. There are many untold tales and secrets around almost every turn in this metropolis. We want to let you know about these five hidden locations.

- ➢ Miradouro Senhora Do Monte.

On Lisbon's tallest hill, in the Graça neighborhood, is where you'll find Miradouro Senhora do Monte. From there, you can take in a breathtaking panorama. Although Lisbon is reputed to have seven hills, this one is not included in that total.

LisbonPortugalTourism.com

➢ Jardim Da Cerca Da Graça

For many years, this park was off-limits to the public. Thankfully, it has since been transformed into a big green space where you can easily spend a day unwinding and taking in the views (of the bridge and the castle!). The park is particularly kid-friendly because it features a tiny playground and a small kiosk that sells food and cool drinks if you (or the kids!) get hungry or thirsty.

➢ Old College Of Young Orphans

To discover the next hidden gem, visit the Mouraria neighborhood. With its delightfully diverse population and ancient buildings, this old town style neighborhood—once a neglected "ghetto"—is today brimming with charm and activity. It's worthwhile to travel there to experience central Lisbon's less commercialized and more genuine side. A police station can be found not far from Martim Moniz Square. Once inside, you'll find the former College of Young Orphans, which is exquisitely decorated with 18th-century tiles depicting various biblical scenarios. It is both a visual pleasure and a crucial piece of Lisbon's past.

- Tasca Do Chico

In reality, Lisbon has two Tasca do Chicos, one in Alfama and one in Bairro Alto. They both have the same concept and are from the same owner. If you enjoy fado, you must visit this location (traditional, melancholic Portuguese music). Here, you may enjoy a meal or light snacks with a fine wine while listening to fado. On Mondays and Wednesdays, the performances begin at 21:00; we advise getting there early to secure a seat. Find Tasca do Chico and other fantastic locations for a drink and some live music by playing our games in Lisbon.

- Jardim Botânico Da Universidade De Lisboa

Need some greenery and fresh air while on your city vacation? For that, the lovely Jardim Botânico da Universidade de Lisboa is ideal. Lisbon's botanical garden, which was first created for scientific objectives, has an amazing variety of plant life. You may completely lose yourself in the tropical atmosphere thanks to their enormous collection of palm trees from around the globe.

THE NATURAL BEAUTIES OF LISBON

Lisbon, which is renowned for its rich history and magnificent architecture, never ceases to astound visitors with its breathtaking scenery and unforgettable natural encounters. Lisbon welcomes visitors wishing to enjoy the outdoors to explore its beaches, natural parks, mountains, and more thanks to its diverse terrains and natural beauties.

- Reserva Natural do Estuário do Tejo

The largest marsh in Portugal is the Reserva Natural do Estuário do Tejo, which is close to the city center. Due to its enormous size, it is the ideal habitat for numerous species, including stilts, pied avocets, spotted redshanks, and common greenshanks. Great for bird and environmental lovers, go in the fall to observe the flamingo population soar. Visitors can also ride on one of the characteristic boats used to cross the river, which are accessible by vehicle, bicycle, or foot.

- Cabo da Roca

This region, which is the most westerly point in all of continental Europe, abruptly descends into the sea from cliffs that tower 140 meters high. Visitors who want to make the most of their visit should go around sunset to witness the sun falling into the sea. The location still uses its 18th-century lighthouse to direct ships safely along the coast.

- Tapada Nacional de Mafra

This open-air park, which was initially created under King Joáo V as a hunting and recreation area, now invites everyone to discover its numerous charms. The park, which spans more than 800 hectares, is home to foxes, rabbits, deer, goats, wild boars, and squirrels, in addition to owls, falcons, and eagles. The park, which is just around 40 kilometers from the city center, also provides sports like crossbow shooting, horseback riding, mountain biking, walking tours, and archery.

➢ Beaches Of Arrábida And Sesimbra

Awe-inspiring beaches are available to visitors along Portugal's border, where coves are formed by the crystal-clear waters. Some of Portugal's most stunning beaches are located south of Lisbon, near Setbal, where visitors may plunge into the azure seas of Praia do Creiro or Portinho da Arrábida. Visitors can take a dolphin-watching boat excursion in Arrábida as well to see the animals splashing in and out of the crystal-clear seas.

- Parque das Nações

This park is a collection of distinctive green areas in Lisbon that include esplanades that look out onto the Tejo River and both native and exotic plants. Take a leisurely stroll through the gardens and see the sculptures by Cutileiro before entering the park's water gardens.

CHAPTER FOUR
EXPERIENCE THE FLAVORS OF LISBON

BEST TRADITIONAL FOOD IN LISBON

No trip is complete without sampling the regional cuisine, and a stroll through Lisbon is an enthralling assault on the senses. There are many meals that are regarded as Lisbon favorites among the diverse, flavorful, and rich Portuguese cuisine. These gastronomic delicacies can be easily found in almost every traditionally run restaurant, and they should not be missed. Additionally, make sure to serve dessert after any of these dishes, including Lisbon's delectable pasteis de nata!

- Bacalhau à brás

Portugal's favorite fish, bacalhau, may be prepared every day of the year without using the same recipe more than once. The majority of eateries provide Bacalhau à brás, which is shredded codfish with fried potatoes, onions, and scrambled eggs, on their menus, despite the seemingly limitless options. Typically, chopped parsley and a sprinkle of black olives are added to the dish's surface. It will be challenging to locate a restaurant in Alfama that doesn't advertise Bacalhau à brás as a special.

- Ameijoas a bulhao pato

One of Lisbon's most well-liked shellfish appetizers is meijoas a bulhao pato. The Portuguese author Raimundo Antonio de Bulhao Pato, who frequented the Lisbon area and frequently praised the meal, is honored by the dish's name. He lived in the 19th century. Clams are cooked in a sauce comprised of white wine, garlic, olive oil, clam juice, or lemon juice in this recipe.

Bread is frequently provided with meejoas a bulhao pato so that it may be dipped into the sauce. The distinctive flavors of this meal are added to other seafood dishes like cod because of its popularity. Ameijoas a bulhao pato is a common item on the menus of coastal and seafood establishments in Lisbon.

- Carne de Porco Alentejana

Pork and clams are two delicacies that the Portuguese love, and Carne de Porco Alentejana is a flavorful fusion of the two. Pork cubes are first marinated in a flavorful sauce made of white wine, paprika, cilantro, garlic, and salt. The pork is then fried, then returned to the marinade with the clams and cooked for an additional few minutes. After the clams have finished cooking and opening, fried, cubed potatoes are added. Some eateries garnish the meal with pickled vegetables, while the majority add freshly chopped cilantro. This Alentejo-inspired cuisine is a local favorite in the city.

- Bifanas (Portuguese pork sandwich)

One of Portugal's most popular street meals is the bifana. Almost every street food cart or booth in the city sells this pork sandwich. Thin slices of pork are marinated in white wine and a lot of garlic before being fried and placed in a crusty bun, making this dish relatively basic but flavorful.

In Lisbon, adding mustard or hot sauce to the sandwich is particularly typical. Bifana is typically savored in the afternoon with a beer, but some cafés also serve it on a plate with fries.

- Polvo à Lagareiro

Similar to fish and clams, povo is a national delicacy that may be prepared in a variety of ways, with Polvo à Lagareiro being one of the most well-known. Polvo da Lagareiro is a straightforward dish that consists of grilled octopus and grilled potatoes with sautéed garlic and olive oil on top. Polvo à Lagareiro literally translates as "octopus with olive oil" because the word "lagareiro" is derived from the manufacturing of olive oil.

- Sardinhas (sardines)

One of Lisbon's finest seafood meals is sardinhas (sardines). The Feast of St. Anthony Sardine Festival in Lisbon is held in mid-June, which is also when they are at their freshest. At this time of year, you can anticipate a fun-filled day with lively celebrations, live music, and sardine food stands.

In some seafood restaurants, the fish is available all year long. Fresh bread is the ideal accompaniment for grilled sardines. Sardinhas in cans are another option, which have become an atypically well-liked souvenir in Lisbon.

- Frango no Churrasco

The Portuguese term for "grilled chicken" or "barbecue chicken" is Franco no Churrasco. It is sometimes referred to as "Chicken Piri-Piri" and is a staple recipe for many restaurants in Portugal and elsewhere. Variations may have their origins in Mozambique and other former Portuguese territories in Africa. In essence, Frango no Churrasco is grilled chicken that has been seasoned with a piri piri spicy sauce. It is typically served with rice, french fries, and a straightforward salad of lettuce, tomato, and onion. The typical beverage pairing with Frango no Churrasco is a small draft beer or a glass of white wine.

- Caldo verde (green soup)

Portugal is known for its famous caldo verde soup, which is frequently served as an appetizer or snack. Almost every neighborhood eatery in and around Lisbon serves it at all times of the day and year. The soup is referred to as "green soup" because its primary components are kale and potatoes. Although sliced chorizo is frequently placed on top, vegetarians can omit it.

Finding a great caldo verde can be challenging, despite being rather straightforward. Even though the recipe doesn't call for dairy or cream, when it's cooked properly, the soup nevertheless tastes creamy. In Lisbon, it's a common late-night snack.

- Caracois

Portuguese people also enjoy eating snails, as does the rest of Latin Europe. From May until late September, signs proclaiming "We have snails" (Há caracóis or temos caracóis) can be seen all throughout Lisbon. Locals react with great enthusiasm to these signs. Served in a butter-garlic broth, caracoles or caracoletas are either sucked out of their shells or fished out with a toothpick. This dish is typically consumed in a social setting, along with a cold beer, while catching up with friends or watching a sporting event on television.

- Cozida a Portuguesa (mixed meat stew)

Traditional Portuguese stew made with meat is known as cozida. The meal is popular among farming families in the little towns surrounding Lisbon. They would use whatever meat and veggies they had on hand to make a stew for everyone to eat. Potatoes, carrots, sausages, cabbage, greens, beans, pork, and beef would frequently be included in this.

This warming stew is flavorful, filling, and full of nutrients. Lisbon's traditional restaurants typically serve it all year long, but the winter is when it is most in demand. In some locations, the stew could even include pig feet and ears.

- Arroz de Marisco

Take a train ride through the nation to see miles of lush, rice-growing fields; the Portuguese have been growing rice for ages, and it is undoubtedly one of their favorite grains. As most people are well aware, seafood plays a significant role in Portuguese cuisine as well. Arroz de Marisco is a dish made of rice and various shellfish. It usually has crab, shrimp, clams, and mussels and is heavily sauced. Piri-piri, garlic, and parsley are traditional Portuguese seasonings. For a small paella variation, some individuals like to add chouriço to their arroz de marisco, but usually it doesn't contain meat from the land.

BEST RESTAURANTS IN LISBON

These outstanding Lisbon eateries are renowned for delivering top-notch cuisine made with locally sourced, fresh ingredients. The city is known for its exceptional seafood dishes, as well as for its traditional desserts and pastries.

As a result of the residents' intense passion for cuisine, Lisbon hosts annual celebrations honoring regional goods. In particular, fresh sardines are honored during a summertime gathering. In addition, there are several top-notch regional wines available to pair with your favorite mouthwatering Portuguese dishes. Given the incredible flavors and excellent value Lisbon has to offer, dining there is a true highlight of any vacation.

- Tasca Da Esquina

Lisbon's Tasca Da Esquina is a cutting-edge cafe-style eatery. It is headed by a chef regarded as the originator of modern Portuguese cuisine. He is deserving of this designation because the petiscos (traditional Portuguese tapas) served here have a contemporary twist. Must-tries include deconstructed bacalhau à brás (salted cod) combined with fried onions and potatoes, as well as octopus salad with sweet potato and coriander.

A 4-, 5-, or 6-course tasting menu of the chef's choices is an option. Keep room in your stomach for the delectable and exquisitely presented desserts from Tasca Da Esquina. The staff speak English and are friendly and well-versed in wine pairings.

Location: Lisbon, Portugal, 1350-119, Rua Domingos Sequeira 41C

Open: Thursday through Monday, from 12.30 to 3:30 and 7.30 to 11 p.m. Tuesday and Wednesday are closed.

- Belcanto

Belcanto provides a classy dining experience in Lisbon because of its imaginative food and fine wines, a lovely and cozy dining area, and attentive service. Enjoy your meal beneath the lofty, vaulted ceilings and modern chandeliers.

Start with some homemade bread that has been freshly cooked and is shaped in a unique way. Hake fish with fig leaf and tuna with edible blossoms are two creative main dishes. There are 6- or 9-course tasting menus offered, with optional wine pairings. Because Belcanto is so well-liked, reservations are strongly advised.

Location: 1200-026 Rua Serpa Pinto, Lisbon, Portugal.

Opening hours are Tuesday through Saturday from 12.30 to 3 pm and from 7 pm to midnight. Sundays and Mondays are closed.

- Eleven

Above Jardim Amália Rodrigues, Eleven is situated in a lovely area. The park, Sao Jorge Castle, and the city of Lisbon are all visible from its enormous windows. You may appreciate excellent service in a spacious, contemporary setting.

Select the truffle tasting menu to enjoy a dessert that features black truffles. A sommelier offers wine pairings that go well with the delectable food. The chef frequently pays a visit and gives diners an autographed recipe book during their meal as a particular touch.

Lisbon, Portugal, Rua Marquês Fronteira Jardim Amália Rodrigues, Parque Eduardo VII, 1070-051

Open: Monday through Saturday from 12:30 to 3:00 and 7:30 to 10:00 p.m.; closed on Sundays.

➢ Taberna da Rua das Flores

Tiny, cozy, and charming, Taberna da Rua das Flores serves fusion cuisine in the form of tapas. Chalkboard menus, shelves stocked with handmade goods, and an old-timey bar atmosphere set the scene.

The chef painstakingly selects fresh market products, resulting in a daily menu that changes every day but is always full of mouthwatering meals. A couple of must-try dishes are goat cheese brulée with figs and fresh oysters with seaweed. Even homegrown olive oil and wines from neighborhood vineyards are sold at Taberna da Rua das Flores. It's important to get there early because this charming restaurant is well-liked yet doesn't accept reservations.

Lisbon, Portugal (1200–1944) 103 Rua das Flores

Opening hours are from midday to 4 p.m. and 6 p.m. to 11:30 p.m., Monday through Saturday. Sundays are closed.

- ➢ Eneko Lisboa

You can eat in a sophisticated dining area at Eneko Lisboa, which is located in a historic factory in Lisbon. The excitement is increased by the open-kitchen design because you can watch the chef and his staff create delectables.

Every meal features creative flavor pairings, such as lobster with coffee butter and purple onion or red mullet fish cooked over charcoal with pepper juice and parsley. Two tasting meals are available at Eneko Lisboa, along with a vast array of exquisite wines.

Location: Lisbon, Portugal, 1300-388, Rua Maria Luisa Holstein 15.

It is open from 7 p.m. to 10:30 p.m. from Tuesday through Saturday; it is closed on Sundays and Mondays.

➢ Bahr Lisboa

Bahr offers traditional regional fare in a spacious eating area with a retro-modern ambiance. Due to the open layout of the kitchen, you can observe the chefs in action. Alternatively, you can reserve a table on the sizable terrace for stunning views of the city and river.

Consider the flavorful grilled squid, runner beans, turnip tops, and seaweed, or the farófias (poached meringue) topped with lemon leaves and cured egg yolks. Save room for the inventive dessert menu from Bahr. The sweet potato or apple sorbet with miso cream is a must-try.

Location: Lisbon, Portugal, Praça Luis de Cames 2, 1200-0243

Hours of operation are 7 am to 11 am, 12 : 30 to 3 : 30, and 7 : 30 to 11 pm on Monday through Friday, and 7 am to 11 am, 12 : 30 to 4 pm, and 7 : 30 to 11 pm on Saturday and Sunday.

- A Praça

A Praça is a portion of the chic LXFactory in Lisbon, where you may wander through modern buildings, cultural activities, and stores. When you are hungry, go to the restaurant for contemporary gourmet fare in a laid-back atmosphere. The design is clean and modern, with an intriguing combination of dark wood, metal, and brick.

You can see everything that is going on in the kitchen thanks to its open layout, and the service is kind and warm. The extensive menu at A Praça will leave you with too many options. The duck legs, the seared tuna salad with tzatziki, and the bunless burgers with cheese, olives, and a fried egg on top are all standouts.

Location: Lisbon, Portugal, Rua Rodrigues de Faria 105, 1300-0501

Open every day from noon to 11 p.m.

➢ Alma Lisboa

Alma is a one-Michelin-star establishment that specializes in avant-garde gourmet cuisine. It's a short stroll away from Lisbon's National Museum of Contemporary Art, making it an excellent choice for dinner after viewing important works of art.

Try one of Alma's creative meat or seafood dishes, such as their take on the popular local delicacy caldeirada or Iberian suckling pig confit (fish and shellfish stew). There is also a "coast to coast" tasting menu that emphasizes fresh fish and seafood from the region. Choose a "out of the box" match to have your meal paired with beer, sake, or wine if you're feeling daring.

Location: Lisbon, Portugal, Rua Anchieta 15, 1200-224

Hours of operation are Tuesday through Sunday, 12.30 to 3.30 and 7 to Midnight (closed on Mondays).

LISBOA POPULAR BARS

Lisbon's nightlife is vibrant but laid-back, just like the overall character of the city. There is a setting to suit your impulsive mood, whether it is a hard-to-find craft beer (Cerveteca Lisboa), an upgraded cocktail in a chic speakeasy setting (Red Frog), or a glass of the nation's famed green wine (BytheWine). Keep our list of the top 15 bars in Lisbon close at hand because they are some of the most enticing places in the city to tie the knot.

- Foxtrot Lisboa

When you go around Lisbon, you'll likely hear the names Alfama, Chiado, and Principe Real. They are not only well-known Lisbon neighborhoods, but the Foxtrot Bar also serves cocktails inspired by them. With its off-the-beaten-path location and Art Deco design, Foxtrot offers a speakeasy atmosphere. You must first ring a bell in order to enter. Given that central heating isn't available in the majority of homes in Lisbon during the winter, a fireplace invites you to sit and be warm. You may enjoy the little courtyard outdoors in the summer. Along with the classics and a large selection of whiskeys and gins, they also offer cocktails with a Lisbon-inspired theme.

Insider's tip: On weekdays from 6 to 9 p.m., there is a happy hour with discounted beer and a unique cocktail.

Location: 28 Travessa Santa Teresa

- The oldest cocktail bar in Lisbon is Pavilho Chinês.

The activities that take place within Pavilho Chinês are difficult to see from the outside, but we invite you to peep inside! Once inside, you won't be able to stop appreciating the tens of thousands of objects on display. On the roof are little airplanes, and there are cupboards full of vintage railways and toy troops. Although it is a pub, you might as well be in a museum. When the proprietors acquired the former grocery shop in 1986, they transformed it into a posh cocktail bar that draws both locals and visitors. A game of pool seems fun. You can play at two tables if you simply go to the rear. You really can't go wrong with the cocktails here, though we do suggest the daiquiris.

Rua Dom Pedro V, number 89.

- By the Wine: For wine enthusiasts

There is a lot of vino available at By the Wine, whether you prefer red, white, or even rosé wine. Simply choose your favorite item from the menu or, if price is not a problem, point to the shelf. One of Portugal's oldest wineries, José Maria da Fonseca, owns the pub. You can order tiny nibbles known as petiscos to go with the delectable Portuguese wine. At Devour Lisbon, we adore the salmon ceviche and the Azeito cheese.

- A Ginjinha

It's likely that anyone you see holding a tiny plastic cup when you're walking around Rossio is sipping gin. Ginjinha, sometimes known as Ginja, may not be simple to pronounce, but it certainly isn't difficult to drink. There is also a Portuguese proverb that translates to "it tastes delicious": "Sabe que nem ginjas." One of the oldest bars in Lisbon where you can purchase this specialty beverage is A Ginjinha. Before pouring it, the proprietors will inquire as to whether you prefer it with cherries or without. We advise purchasing ginjinha com elas for an added kick. You may taste the fruit itself in addition to the taste of the beverage.

Location: 8 Largo San Domingos.

➢ Loucos e Sonhadores

In contrast to the majority of bars in Bairro Alto, this one does not have flamboyant outdoor signs advertising shots and cocktails.

Loucos e Sonhadores, which translates to Madmen and Dreamers, is a place where the little things matter most. Locals go to this laid-back venue for the free salty popcorn and a beer or glass of wine. If you must know, they do indeed serve cocktails. Unlike most of the bars in the region, this one features lots of seating options and a unique interior design. Just remember to be there early.

Location: 261 Rua da Rosa

➢ Fábrica Musa

Visit Fábrica Musa for a sample of Lisbon's craft beer. One of the three breweries that settled in Marvila, currently known as Lisbon's beer quarter, is Musa. Sagres or Super Bock were the only two lagers that could be found on tap prior to the emergence of craft beer. But that is now over! You may now finally enjoy a variety of beers, from the hoppy IPA to the coffee-flavored stout, thanks to establishments like Musa.

➢ Trobadores Lisboa.

Trobadores isn't your typical pub in Lisbon. You'll be transported to the Middle Ages by this welcoming tavern. Drinks are served in horns and folk music is playing in the background because, well, why not? You can also buy them in a terracotta cup if you're not able to manage that. The tap beers or hidromel, a traditional Portuguese mead, are typically ordered by locals. Live performances by folk groups are occasionally invited, which enhances the ambiance even more.

27 Rua So Julio

➢ Quiosque Príncipe Real

Though technically not a bar, you must visit at least one kiosk while you're in Lisbon. They are scattered across the city, but the Quiosque Prncipe Real is our favorite. This tiny kiosk, located close to the Principe Real garden, is the ideal spot for an afternoon beer or a coffee. Here, you may also get little treats like the custard tarts from Lisbon.

➢ TOPO Martim Moniz

From a distance, you can make out the word "BAR" in red neon, but how do you enter this rooftop bar in Lisbon? Simple. Go through the mall. You did read that correctly. You enter the mall, use the elevator, and six levels later, TOPO is where you are. Even just the vistas are worth the trip! With a martini in hand, you can see the San Jorge Castle and several of Lisbon's vantage points from here. There is frequently music being played by a DJ, and the drinks are even given song names. The Material Girl, a vodka-based cocktail with a hint of strawberry and lemon, is one of our favorites.

Address: 6th Floor, Centro Comercial Martim Moniz

➢ Casa Independente Lisbon

Largo do Intendente now has new life thanks to Casa Independente. What was once a run-down section of the city is today one of Lisbon's hippest districts.

More than just a bar, Casa Independente is. It combines the functions of an art gallery, a concert hall, and a cultural association. There are other places inside where you can relax with a drink, or you can go straight to their terrace filled of vegetation, which is shown in the article's opening image!

Keep an eye on their website to stay informed about any great events.

Location: 45 Largo do Intendente Pina

EXPLORE LISBON'S MARKET

Lisbon has various fantastic markets, including those for fruits and vegetables, crafts, and fleas. Therefore, there is a market in Lisbon that is ideal for you, whether you're wanting to buy some fish for supper, a handmade gift for someone's birthday, or a book in Portuguese to help you learn the language Lisbon has held markets for many years, and they are still an important aspect of daily life there. At food markets, locals and visitors mix with celebrity chefs; at vintage clothing fairs, customers haggle over jackets and jewelry; and at flea markets, DJs compete with record collectors for rare records.

Set aside a few hours to get the best deals because many of Lisbon's biggest and best markets fill large historic buildings or take over entire neighborhoods. There is typically a nice selection of lunch pit stops with great local street delicacies and inexpensive cold drinks..

- ➢ Mercado da Ribeira (fresh market).

The biggest market in Lisbon is called Mercado da Ribeira. Although the majority of people only know it for the Time Out Food Market, which is Lisbon's largest food market, it is also home to one of the city's biggest fresh food markets.

The Mercado da Ribeira has avoided the trap of turning into an expensive farmer's market despite being in the city center and close to the Time Out Market. Instead, it's a daily market that sells almost everything on your shopping list for a very low price. Here, in one of Lisbon's most well-known marketplaces, you can get anything from fruit and vegetables to fish, meat, and spices.

ABERTO
TODOS OS DIAS
MERCADO
DA RIBEIRA

- ➢ Time Out Market Lisboa.

The Time Out Market, Lisbon's largest food hall, houses some of the city's top pubs and eateries under one roof. This area is home to several of Lisbon's most well-known restaurants, making it a great place to taste a single dish without having to place an order for the entire dinner.

Manteigaria, a company that produces some of the top pastéis de nata in Lisbon, is also housed in the Mercado da Ribeira building. They might even surpass Pastéis de Belém's pastéis de natas in quality. On Av. 24 de Julho, directly across from the Cais do Sodré train station, lies Manteigaria, which is at the front of the structure. Location: Av. 24 de Julho 49, Lisboa, Portugal, 1200-479

Open every day from 10:00am till 12:00am

➢ Feira do Relógio.

One of the major Sunday street markets in the city, Feira do Relógio, is a beautiful location where you can get amazing prices on just about anything you can think of. Although this market is a little off the main path and located in a peaceful residential area, the trek is worthwhile because it is close to the Metro line. Among the vendor stalls, you may discover anything from fresh flowers and fruit to antiques and collectibles, vintage clothing, and even electronics and gadgets. Even furniture and household items are available here.

This market is where you're likely to locate any buried riches if you're hunting for them. The distance to the north of the city center is only 18 minutes.

Address: 1950-011 Av. Santo Condestável WC, Lisboa, Portugal

Open: every Sunday from 6 a.m. to 3 p.m. (closed Monday–Saturday).

➢ Mercado Praça da Figueira

The ancient Mercado Praça da Figueira offers all the charm of the past along with the best contemporary products, fresh delicacies, and prepared foods, ranging from meats and cheese to coffee. The market, which specialized in farm-fresh fruits and vegetables, started in 1755 in an abandoned hospital building and swiftly rose to become Lisbon's main market. When a national corporation restored it in 2013, it experienced a rebirth that preserved all the elegance of its historical heritage while giving it a decidedly contemporary presentation and product options.

Today, it has a coffee shop, a butcher, a deli, fish, fruits, and vegetables, and a wine cellar. Additionally, it's right in the middle of the city.

Lisboa, Portugal's Praça da Figueira 10, 1100-240

Open from 8.30 am to 8 pm, Monday through Saturday (closed on Sundays).

➢ Mercado Biológico do Principe Real

This fantastic food market, which specializes in farm-fresh and organic vegetables, is open every Saturday from 8 am to 2 pm in the super-hip, extremely affluent district of Prncipe Real (as well as handicrafts and bric-a-brac). You can expect to find mouthwatering foods that you can bring home as gifts, such homemade cakes, organic wine, local honeys, and cheeses. Additionally, there are stalls brimming with produce, Instagrammable cut flowers, and fruit.

- LxFactory Sunday Market.

The LxFactory Sunday Market is one of Lisbon's more well-known flea markets. It is located in a bohemian area that draws a youthful, trendy population and sells vintage goods, arts, and crafts. This weekly market is hidden among a row of upscale stores, eateries, and cafes. The market itself is a terrific place to find pre-owned treasures, including artwork, collectibles, antiques, and other rare items. Old-fashioned clothing, vintage vinyl, and wall art are all available. A variety of gifts, trinkets, and handcrafted arts and crafts are also available.

For farm-fresh food, it is also coupled with a nearby fresh fruit and vegetable market. From the city center to the west, it takes roughly 30 minutes.

Location: 1300-501 Lisboa, Portugal, R. Rodrigues de Faria 103

Hours of operation on Sunday are 11 am to 8 pm (closed Monday–Saturday).

➢ Mercado De Santa Clara Lisboa.

The Mercado de Santa Clara started out selling food next to the large Feira da Ladra flea market in the narrow lanes of the old Alfama neighborhood. Since then, a center for culinary arts and nearby shops selling crafts and antiques have joined it. There will undoubtedly be treats for an outside meal. In the tiny park in front of the Santa Engrácia Church (also known as the National Pantheon), put up your picnic after visiting the Sao Vicente de Fora Church to admire the exquisitely tiled interior.

Location: 1100-472 Lisboa, Portugal, Campo de Santa Clara

Tuesday and Saturday from 9 am to 6 pm (closed Wednesday–Friday and Sunday–Monday).

➢ Avenida Da Liberdade Flea Market.

The magnificent, tree-lined Avenida da Liberdade in Lisbon is frequently compared to Paris' Champs-Élysées, and its well-liked flea market is located beneath upscale retailers like Prada and Armani. The best personal shoppers concur that among the well-polished antiques, used books, and sought-after collectibles are a ton of great deals. Just don't be shy about bartering; it's customary.

alamy
Image ID: KX5GDD
www.alamy.com

CHAPTER FIVE
LOCATION SETTLING IN LISBON

IS LISBON OFFERING VACATION ACCOMMODATIONS?

Discover the nicest vacation homes we have to offer. A house creates a home.

- *Villa Domingues.*

Villa Domingues in Lisbon offers accommodations with air conditioning and access to a garden, 1.9 kilometers from Rossio and 1.9 kilometers from the Dona Maria II National Theatre.

St. George's Castle is 4.9 kilometres from the villa, while Commerce Square is 4.4 km away. At a distance of 8 kilometres from Villa Domingues, Humberto Delgado Airport is the closest airport. The lovely home of Villa Domingues is quite enjoyable. There is lots of room in the house and a beautiful yard. It takes 20 to 30 minutes to walk (or take the metro) to the city center.

- *Villa With 3 Bedrooms In The Heart Of Lisbon*

This 3-bedroom villa in central Lisbon, 3.4 kilometers from Rossio and 3.9 km from Miradouro da Senhora do Monte, offers free WiFi, air conditioning, a garden, and a terrace. Access to a balcony is provided by this building. The villa has a lot of room. Lots of excellent restaurants nearby. Definitely suggested.

➢ *Pool-Equipped Luxury Home In Lisbon*

This luxury villa with a pool in Lisbon provides accommodations with free WiFi, air conditioning, an outdoor swimming pool, and a terrace. It is located in Lisbon, 7.2 kilometers from Luz Football Stadium and 2 kilometers from Jeronimos Monastery. Private parking is free, and there is a garden and a pool at this home. The house's design and the pool are wonderful. There was a lot of room, and it was really quiet. It's like a home away from home.

➢ *The Lisbonne Collection's Garden Mansion In Historic Center 4*

The vacation home has five bedrooms, a satellite TV, a washer and dryer, a kitchen with a dishwasher and a microwave, and two bathrooms with showers. The vacation house includes linens and towels. stunning residence that exudes Portuguese culture and spirit. Sao Vincente is the location

➢ *Quinta do Boição*

A flat-screen TV and a private bathroom with a hairdryer, complimentary toiletries, and a shower are provided in the vacation rental. Additionally, some of the apartments have kitchens with a fridge, an oven, and a microwave. There was no breakfast provided, but overall it was a fantastic stay in a serene location that was perfect for your trip's last few restful days.

> ➢ *Warm Duplex Residence in the Heart of Lisbon*

The Cozy Duplex House in Downtown Lisbon is located in the Misericordia neighborhood of Lisbon, 1.1 kilometers from Ribeira Market, 1.2 kilometers from the Dona Maria II National Theatre, and 1.2 kilometers from Rossio. Both the Jeronimos Monastery and the Luz Football Stadium are 5 miles apart from this vacation home.

PROS AND DRAWBACKS OF EXPAT LIVING IN LISBON

Living in Almada, which is close to Lisbon, is a terrific idea because it's simple to travel around by car or public transportation. Portugal has high living expenses, particularly when compared to the US. The locals are welcoming and cordial. Although often dull, the cuisine is good. However, I do believe it to be healthier for your health: "One foreigner in Lisbon explained.

It's simple to live here thanks to the generally excellent weather and easy access to goods and services. Naturally, COVID has had an impact on everything, which has made things more challenging. Accessible and inexpensive healthcare is available. Although it has taken longer to learn, English is frequently understood. It's crucial that there are many outdoor activities available, such as cycling, hiking, and water sports. There is a lot of history to discover as well as old world charm. This location is beneficial since it has easy access to other parts of Europe. I lived in various Asian nations in the past. Additionally, Europe is nearer to the US, making return trips more feasible, "a different expat in Lisbon stated."

Portugal is a wonderfully organized country where everyone respects one another. In most retail stores and medical facilities, you take a number and wait for your turn. I really enjoy this element of life here. Nobody attempts to skip a cue. Additionally, most people are really kind and helpful to one another. The government bureaucracy is the one issue I consistently hear complaints about. But once more, in my experience, you just have to wait for your turn or your number to be called, "said another foreigner in Lisbon.

There isn't much to dislike, so let's start there. Graffiti is prevalent in Lisbon. In many ways, it takes away from the city's attractiveness, but with time, you learn to look past it and appreciate the other features. Portuguese motorists drive aggressively and impatiently. Their personal space is smaller than it is in America, including the street cars. The adjustment process takes time. If you purchase a property, don't anticipate any required upgrades to be finished as soon as in the United States. The nice things include the pleasant weather, the country's diversified landscape, the bread and wine, and the friendliness of its residents toward outsiders (in this country, being friendly to someone does not necessarily mean inviting them into your home). The literature (another reason to learn the language), the comedy (again, language), the rich culture, and the general demeanor of the Portuguese (they are very slow to anger and are far less prone to violence than Americans), among other things, may take a good friend or acquaintance some time to invite you into their home. A final word about language learning: One may succeed and enjoy a lot of things here even without speaking the language. "You can take advantage of everything the nation has to offer if you have a thorough understanding of it," a foreigner residing in Lisbon explained.

Some of the world's best coffee (and at 0.65-0.70 euros, cheap). The breads are of excellent quality, delectable, and a reasonable price. The wines (I exclusively consume red) are very good; you can go into practically any store and purchase a bottle for between two and three euros, and it will be excellent. The transportation system is more or less dependable and typically good. Another foreign national residing in Lisbon, Portugal, said: "If you're over 65, a monthly pass costs just 20 euros, and you may travel very far with it."

In November 2016, we bought a condo in Cascais, Portugal, which is a suburb of Lisbon. We adore the village's atmosphere, cuisine, climate, and history. When we wish to visit the lovely city of Lisbon, we can take a quick train ride (40 minutes) to the large city before returning to the peace and quiet of our home in Cascais. After leaving the USA, there is a sense of relief and we feel extremely safe here in Portugal. Since we arrived, we haven't encountered any wahoo, open-carrying nuts outside of TV. Neither of us speaks much Portuguese, but 95% of the time that doesn't matter. When it does, we utilize translation applications to get by. The quality of healthcare is excellent and the cost of living is fantastic, "another foreigner in Lisbon said.

BENEFIT OF LIVING IN LISBON

The weather, social scene, and cost of living in comparison to other European capitals top my list of pros. The difficult cobblestone streets, numerous steps, paperwork, and bureaucracy all drawbacks, though. I hope my list of advantages and disadvantages is useful.

- Lisbon has a significantly higher cost of living than in other European cities like London or Paris.
- Excellent expat and digital nomad scene.
- Excellent weather may be found in Lisbon during 10 out of the 12 months of the year. Only December and January are truly dull and can get chilly indoors at night, but the weather in Lisbon is a huge improvement over that of the UK.
- Because there is such a vibrant foreign community in Lisbon, English is commonly spoken and is generally easy to understand.
- Head over to Pink Street's sports bars and karaoke for a great social experience.
- Take the train at Cais do Sodre to Carcevelos (half an hour) or Cascais for a quick trip to the beach (just under an hour).
- Good business opportunities—many options to network, including tech and freelancer meetups.
- You are on UK time, or GMT, which is fantastic for anyone who freelances for UK companies or who still works for a UK employer.

DRAWBACKS OF LIVING IN LISBON

- Oh, there are so many steps. This will result in it taking you 20 minutes longer to go from point A to point B in

Lisbon, especially if you choose to stroll through Alfama.

- Put your high heels away since Lisbon's cobblestone streets aren't made for fashion!
- Apartments are more common than houses, but this has drawbacks, including noise from above and below and having to climb stairs every time you get home.
- Things can take some time. For example, it took me three days to open a bank account after going in and waiting for a few hours at a time. When I started my account with ActivoBank Lisbon, they were incredibly helpful and spoke excellent English.
- It might be expensive to eat and drink in some areas of the tourist and historical centers (but you quickly learn where to go).
- Renting can be difficult because many troublesome landlords refuse to make repairs and withhold your security deposit for no apparent reason.

Compared to other areas of Portugal, renting and buying property is expensive.

- The insides of many Portuguese apartments are freezing during the winter since they were designed to withstand the summer's heat. In the winter, it can get unbearably cold inside some flats.
- In an official position, such as the Financas or Town Hall for residency, the language barrier can be difficult. When you need to apply for a D7 Visa, however, things can get complicated with CRUE.
- There are some cultural differences that will require some getting used to. For instance, couvert-even bread

and cheese that you didn't purchase will be charged as starters in restaurants!

CHAPTER SIX
CONCLUSION

OBSERVING COVID-19 PROTOCOLS IN LISBON.

Important Information for Lisbon Travelers.

- Before going to Lisbon, make sure you are COVID-19-vaccinated.
- Avoid traveling to Lisbon if you haven't received your COVID-19 vaccinations in a timely manner because you might find it difficult to get medical care there.
- You may still be susceptible to contracting and spreading COVID-19 even if your vaccinations against it are current.
- Anyone over the age of two needs to properly wear a quality mask in indoor public areas.
- Even if you have had all of your COVID-19 vaccinations, your doctor should be informed if you have a compromised immune system or are more likely to get a serious illness. You may choose to postpone your trip to Lisbon if necessary.
- In Lisbon, abide by all rules and suggestions.

What You Must Understand:

- Avoid COVID-19 to protect yourself and others:
- Before you travel, make sure your COVID-19 vaccinations are current.
- Before you travel, think about being tested.

- Observe the CDC's guidelines for mask use when traveling and using public transportation.
- After a trip, get tested.
- Before departing the United States, research the COVID-19 situation and travel restrictions for your destination. Each nation may have its own requirements for entering and leaving.
- Non-citizens and non-immigrants: Before boarding your journey to Lisbon, you must provide documentation proving that you have received the entire primary series of an authorized COVID-19 vaccine. There are very few exceptions.

Prior to Departure from the United States

- Plan ahead if necessary.
- Before you travel, make sure your COVID-19 vaccinations are current.
- Find out where to receive a vaccine or booster and when you can get your booster.
- Especially for those who have been boosted, COVID-19 vaccinations are beneficial against preventing major illness, hospitalization, and even death.
- Verify the COVID-19 condition there right now.
- Follow all instructions from transportation providers (such as airlines, cruise lines, and bus companies) and any instructions from the location, such as wearing a mask or providing proof of immunization or testing.
- Other nations' requirements could be different from American requirements. You risk being denied

admission and being forced to return to the United States if you don't adhere to the rules of your destination.

- Even if you have had all of your COVID-19 vaccinations, you need take additional precautions to protect yourself from the virus if you have a compromised immune system or are at higher risk for serious illness.
- Before you travel, discuss your risk with your healthcare professional and think about postponing your trip to places with high COVID-19 levels. Even if you are current, you should be aware of the necessary safety measures.
- Learn how to protect them if you plan to visit someone who is more likely to contract COVID-19 and become really ill.

Printed in Great Britain
by Amazon

38031428R00099